PUFFIN STORY BOOKS

Edited by Eleanor Graham

PS 75

TO SCHOOL IN THE SPANISH MAIN

ALICE BERRY-HART

This thrilling story of mystery and adventure in wartime starts in New York Harbour, aboard a cargo boat bound for the West Indies in which a number of children are being evacuated from wartime England, among them four boys, whose ages range from eight to fourteen.

They sail in convoy, are torpedoed almost within sight of their destination – and that is only the beginning of a deep and sinister plot. The island offers unlimited swimming and sailing on the lagoon, picnics among the coconut groves, and such delights, but the four English boys find themselves too closely involved in some unpleasant happenings to give their whole minds to the lighter side of school life.

This is a first story by a new author. It makes its first appearance in print in the Puffin series. For boys and girls from 9 to 15.

ALICE BERRY-HART

TO SCHOOL IN THE SPANISH MAIN

*

ILLUSTRATED BY
RICHARD KENNEDY

PENGUIN BOOKS
MELBOURNE · LONDON · BALTIMORE

First Published 1953

TO

DAVID

*Made and printed in Great Britain
for Penguin Books Ltd
Harmondsworth, Middlesex
by Wyman & Sons Ltd
London, Reading, and Fakenham*

CONTENTS

1 The Start of the Voyage   7

2 A Search in the Black-out   27

3 Straws Show Which Way the Wind Blows   30

4 Torpedoed Within Sight of Land   51

5 Confusion and Doubt   61

6 The Mystery Deepens   72

7 Exploring the Island   82

8 Swimming   93

9 Pat is Found   105

10 The Secret Band   112

11 What Really Happened   120

12 Jason Picks up the Threads   134

13 A Secret Event with a Surprising Outcome   142

14 Jason Wishes He Had Gone to the Picnic   154

15 A Case of Mistaken Identity   165

16 The Special Messenger Seeks Advice   171

17 Who is the Spy?   181

18 A Strange Trip in a Speed-boat   187

19 The Mystery Solved   196

LIST OF ILLUSTRATIONS

'Cut along you two,' said Jason 13

Our friends of the American Red Cross have sent a
box of presents for you' 21

Andrew ran by banging the gong 32

They all took their places at the sound of the boat
drill alarm 43

The explosion was terrific 49

Half-dazed with heat he carried Pat across his
shoulder 55

'There's someone lying down in the cart,' said
Andrew 70

Between mouthfuls Andrew gave a stirring account
of the torpedoing of the ship 84

'Hi, you've dropped the paper,' Andrew shouted 89

'What about the examination, Mr Solomon?' 103

Jason disliked Mr Boomhill at sight 122

John saw Goldbeard with a box in his hands 137

Mr Jones found another leaf when he was
shaving 143

Jason stopped and looked round, and the negroes
stopped too 161

On the beach at Coconut Reach 172

'Is it important?' asked Lady May 177

They could see three people standing by the trees 193

Three men came wading across the channel 199

CHAPTER I

The Start of the Voyage

'YOU'LL find your boys somewhere on deck,' the Purser shouted though the window of his office. 'Here's the list: Jason Foster, John Dawe, Andrew Thomson, and Pat Duncan. Their kit has been checked, and is in their cabin. Number 58, aft, on this deck. You are in number 60.' Though he was not three feet away Mrs Grant could scarcely hear him above the clatter of machinery on deck, and the clumping of feet along the corridors. She clutched at the paper which the Purser shoved towards her, and gently pushing her little son and daughter forward with her suitcases, made her way with difficulty back through the crowded ship.

At the foot of the main companionway a thin, small boy with enormous ears and black-rimmed spectacles sat on the banisters, watching the throng of passengers, soldiers, New York Harbour Police, and members of the crew as they surged up and down the stairs. The boy wore his life-jacket already adjusted, and had an armlet sewn on to his left sleeve. Mrs Grant glanced at her list. Andrew Thomson, aged nine. She chanced it.

'Andrew!' she called. The boys large ears seemed to waggle. His spectacles turned in her direction; he gave a wide, friendly grin, and swarmed down from his perch. He was as thin as a monkey.

'Yes, I'm Andrew Thomson,' he said, showing his armlet.

'I'm Mrs Grant.'

'Oh yes: you're to be in charge of us, aren't you?'

'I am. Can you tell me where my cabin is? Number 60.'

'This way,' Andrew said with an air of happy importance. He seized her bag with both hands, and lugged it beside her. 'Right at the back here – the last one,' he said.

Number 60 was a mere slit: a sort of corridor end which had been partitioned off and almost filled with two bunks, one above the other.

'It's very small,' Andrew said, backing out and letting the lady in.

'Never mind how small it is,' Mrs Grant said thankfully. 'The great thing is that I haven't got to share it with strangers. Coming across the Atlantic I was in with ten others.'

'There were twenty of us,' Andrew said. 'And I was the sickest of the lot. I was so sick . . .'

'Now I'd better shove the suitcases under the bunk here,' Mrs Grant said hastily, 'and then perhaps I should find the other boys in my care.'

'Our cabin is just here,' Andrew said throwing open the door of number 58.' It was very small, but had four bunks in it.

'You'll have to take turns dressing,' Mrs. Grant said.

'Coming across in the Atlantic Convoy we didn't undress,' Andrew said in excited tones. 'We slept in our things, with our life-belts on.'

'You all came together to New York from Liverpool, didn't you?'

'Yes we did, though we didn't know each other before. We're all going to the West Indies, to Badanda College, you know.'

A sound in the cabin made Mrs Grant look behind the door. A boy stood there. He had a round, close-cropped head, a chubby face completely devoid of expression, and blue eyes steadily fixed on Mrs Grant.

'Well!' exclaimed that lady. 'Would this be . . .' she glanced at her list. 'Would this be Pat Duncan?'

'Oh, yes, that's Pat all right,' Andrew said cheerfully.

'I'm Mrs Grant, Pat,' she explained. 'This is my son Guy. He is not quite two. And this is Jean, who is four. And I am going to have charge of you, and Andrew, and two other boys. Won't I have a large family?'

Pat stared at her without speaking.

'Andrew's going to take us up to find Jason and John,' Mrs Grant continued. 'Don't you want to come with us?'

'No,' said Pat, not moving from his corner.

'But you don't want to stay here all by yourself?' Mrs Grant urged.

'Yes, I do.'

'Don't mind him,' Andrew said, 'He's like that. But he's all right really.'

'But why won't you come with us?' Mrs Grant said, looking distressed.

'I know where I am here,' the boy said not stirring. 'There are too many people in the corridors. I might get lost.'

'But I could hold your hand.'

'You've already got two people by the hand,' the boy said, indicating Guy and Jean.

'Then come with me, fathead!' Andrew shouted impatiently.

'No. I want to stay here.'

'It's no use,' Andrew said. 'When we're at sea he'll be all right. He was just like this when we left Liverpool. He's O.K. Come on.'

'Where are the others?'

'They're on deck. Look, we won't shove through that crowd again. Let's go this way.' He stepped over a high, brass-bound threshold, pushed aside some canvas curtains, and emerged upon the well deck, closely followed by the others. Here the noise was deafening. Large wooden crates were being lifted from the dock and lowered down through the hatches. Winches were grinding and cargo bumping.

'You see that huge ship opposite, with all those decks?' Andrew asked excitedly. 'Well, that's the one we came on from England. We only had to walk round the three sides of this dock, and come aboard.'

'You must have had hundreds and hundreds of passengers,' Mrs Grant said.

'Millions,' Andrew grinned. 'And most of them children. But none of the others are coming our way. They are staying here in the States or going up to Canada. Look, there are our two boys, standing at the rail up there. The tall one's Jason, and the fat one's John.' He scrambled up the starboard ladder to the upper deck, and Mrs Grant followed with her children.

The two older boys were looking across the narrow strip of water at the imposing vessel tied at the opposite wharf. At Andrew's shout they both looked round.

'Hi! She's here!' Andrew called. The taller boy affected not to hear, but he stroked his fair hair with a self-conscious gesture as he turned his gaze back to the large ship. His fat, dark-haired companion looked as if he felt he should advance to meet the lady.

'I say, Jason,' he murmured, 'it must be Mrs Grant. She's got red hair, and she has a couple of red-haired infants, so I suppose they are hers.'

'In short,' Jason returned in a bitter undertone, 'we have the complete school, from the Kindergarten to the Senior House.'

'Don't be a chump. Turn round! She's coming to speak to us.'

'Oh crumbs, she would!'

'Well, here we are,' Mrs Grant exclaimed brightly, shaking hands. 'So that's the ship you came over in? We were in a much smaller one, I'm thankful to say.'

'Were you in the same convoy?' John asked politely.

'I think so. We came out to meet you from Glasgow.'

'We saw your ships join on,' Andrew chimed in. 'But we were in the middle line all the way, just behind the Commodore.'

'We saw you. Well, if you don't mind, I'll go down and do some unpacking. And Guy needs a rest.'

'Let me stay on deck, Mummie,' Jean begged.

'All right, if the boys don't mind, and if you don't climb up on the rail.'

'I'll take her around and show her the ship,' Andrew said.

'Would you like any help with baggage or anything?' John asked.

'No, I can manage; but it's very kind of you,' Mrs Grant returned. 'And perhaps Jason, as you're the oldest, you'd cast an eye in the direction of the infants when they are on this side of the deck.'

When she had gone, and Andrew and Jean had disappeared through the door of the smoking room, the two older boys once more resumed their examination of the neighbouring ship which they had so recently left. A loud speaker on her began to issue instructions.

'Passengers from A to J,' the voice said, 'will proceed to D Deck to the Purser's Office. Those who have not received information about their luggage will now have an opportunity to see the steward about it in room 100. Passengers from K to Z may now have tea in the lounge on B deck. Let me repeat that no children are allowed on A deck.'

'All passengers whose names begin with O,' Jason proclaimed in an unctuous imitation of the loud speaker, 'will take their left feet in their right hands and hop around B deck five times.'

'While those between Q and V,' John went on, 'will climb the mainmast backwards.'

'Infants under 95,' Jason continued, 'will kindly remove beards before listening to the children's hour in the nursery which is next door to the Captain's biscuit.' Both boys laughed immoderately at their own jokes, but their amusement was checked abruptly by the hearty laughter of Andrew and Jean who had returned unperceived, and had been listening with appreciation.

'Cut along you two,' Jason said in a voice which was rougher than he had intended because it kept breaking into a hoarse baritone.

'Jacko, you monkey,' John added, 'take your charge over to the other side.'

'It's not your private deck,' Andrew retorted with perfect good humour. Once more the loud speaker blared out.

'Will Mr H. H. Smith please report to the purser's office', it said. 'Mr H. H. Smith. Report to the Purser's office please.'

'Will the lady who dropped a million gold sovereigns in the well deck please count her change more carefully next time,' Jason announced. Andrew's shrill laugh was echoed by Jean's.

'Do you think there's a chance of their hearing you?' Andrew asked.

'Who cares?' Jason asked.

'I'm glad we're not on board her now, aren't you?' Andrew continued. 'This is freer, and there's not such a crowd.'

'It's quite as crowded for its size, you stupe,' John said.

'But still,' Andrew persisted, 'it's going to be more fun on this ship. We can go wherever we like.'

'Try going up to the bridge deck,' suggested Jason.

'Well, if you can go wherever you like, why don't you go?' John said craftily. 'Look, go to the stern and have a talk with the gunners. If we see you there we'll know that you are allowed there, see?'

'Righto! Come on Jean,' Andrew said with alacrity. The two children set off at full speed.

'That's a relief,' sighed Jason.

'I say, Jass old son, do you think we'll all have to share a table? ' John asked.

'What, with all those kids?'

'Oh, I suppose we will, since we're all in Mrs. Grant's care.'

'I'd rather starve!'

'Passengers are warned,' the loud speaker broke out again, 'that life-jackets must be carried at all times. The loss of a jacket must be reported to the chief officer at once. Passengers are reminded that no smoking is allowed on deck.'

'They must be getting ready to go,' John said. 'Wonder if they'll leave again before we do; and where'll they be going?'

'Cut along, you two,' said Jason

'Perhaps they'll be in our convoy,' Jason suggested. He looked gloomily at the vessel which had brought them all away from the country they loved.

'I shouldn't think so, or they wouldn't have taken the trouble to change us over to this tub.'

'They might be going the same way at first, and then through the Panama Canal. It's not likely that a big ship like that would call at a speck of an island like Tripadoes.'

'I wonder where the other fellows are,' John said. 'On the train by now, I suppose, those who are going to Canada.'

'Shut up,' Jason muttered. 'Why didn't my father know the headmaster of a Canadian school instead of one in the West Indies? I love winter sports ... If we *had* to be evacuated ...'

'The bathing there ought to be pretty good,' John reminded him. 'And you know, there were piles of pirates in the Spanish Main. I think it will be rather exciting.'

'Exciting? A small school like Banana College?'

'Badanda College, you fathead!' chirped Andrew appearing suddenly on the rail beside him.

'What, back again?' groaned Jason and John.

'Did you see me talking to the gunners? They're going to show me how to use the anti-aircraft guns.'

'Oh yeah?' Jason scoffed.

'What have you done with Jean?' John asked.

'She wanted to go back to her mother. She's only four.'

'Grand time we'll have in Banana College with little playmates like Monkey here, and Pat, and Jean and the Grant baby to play ring-a-rosy with,' Jason muttered.

'Mrs Grant is going to teach in the school,' Andrew announced.

'How do you know, Monkey?'

'Because she told me. And it's quite a big school. I think she'll be a nice teacher, don't you?'

'Won't matter what I think. She's not likely to take our class, unless they put us all in the kindergarten.'

'But she doesn't teach kindergarten,' Andrew said.

'How do you know?'

'Because I asked her.'

'Oh, you did, did you? And what did she say she taught?'

'She says she hasn't taught much.'

'Huh!' Jason gave what he meant to be a scornful grunt, which changed into an upper register halfway, and made Andrew laugh. 'Well, cut along and don't bother us,' Jason concluded, trying to help Andrew on his way with the point of his shoe.

'Go and ask her what she does teach,' John suggested.

'I don't have to.'

'All right, don't.'

'Because I have already asked her,' Andrew cried triumphantly. 'And do you know what she said she was?'

'A cook,' John murmured idly.

'Or a milliner,' Jason said.

'No. Both wrong, fatheads. She said that she was a geographer.'

'A what?'

'A geographer. You should know what that is at your ages,' Andrew said perkily.

'A geographer! Rats! She means she teaches Geography to infants,' John said, yawning.

'Give all the rivers of Asia Minor which flow into the Pacific,' Jason said in a falsetto whisper.

'Well, you're both wrong,' Andrew sang out. 'I know, because I asked her all about it.'

'I suppose you asked her to tell you the story of her life,' John marvelled.

'Well, I did ask her some friendly questions,' Andrew admitted. 'She said that she was going to teach geography at Badanda College.'

'But I thought you said she said she wasn't a teacher,' Jason growled. 'One minute you say one thing, and then you say another.'

'You listen carefully, and you'll learn much,' Andrew said. 'I only said that she hadn't taught before.'

'Well what did she do, then?'

'I think she drew maps for atlases, or made weather

charts for the radio, or something. Anyhow, she'll be very useful, because there's no map of our route on the boat, and she will be able to tell us where we are every day, and how near we are to the different islands.'

'Huh!' growled Jason.

'Any old how,' Andrew said, 'if we're torpedoed I'm jolly well going to be on the same raft as her.'

'Why?' John asked.

'Because she could draw a chart and tell us the nearest way to land.'

'Well, you're not likely to be on a raft, but in a life-boat,' John said.

'We're in the same boat, anyhow,' Andrew said triumphantly. 'Our names are all down for boat 5, and that's the second one along there.' He swung around, and the point of his elbow landed on the waistcoat of a burly man in uniform who had come up followed by a large red-headed, red-bearded man with twinkling blue eyes.

'Steady!' remonstrated the officer after an involuntary grunt. 'Right on the mark, that was!'

'Sorry, Captain,' Andrew gulped. Even his cheeky friendliness quailed before such an incident. Jason took his foot off the rail and drew himself up to his full height. John stood with his habitual serene and rather indolent smile.

'Well, all settled comfortably?' the Captain asked.

'Yes, sir,' Andrew piped up. 'I have the top bunk by the door.'

'You have, eh? Well, you are all bound for Tripadoes, eh? Nice little island. I suppose you can all swim, eh?'

'Yes, sir!' said Jason and John. For once Andrew could not shout out first. He wriggled, bit his lips, touched his spectacles, and then said,

'I can almost float in my bath.'

The Captain and the red-bearded man roared with laughter.

'You'll learn,' the Captain said. 'Lots of swimming there, eh, Dix? And sailing, too. You ask Dix here. He'll tell you all about it.'

'Is it a coral island, sir?' John asked.

'Partly,' the red-bearded man said. 'It's different from the other West Indian Islands. Part of it is white coral, and flat; and part of it is volcanic and hilly. Funny little place, but you'll like it. All going to Badanda College, eh?'

'We call it Banana College,' Andrew giggled.

'None of you been there before, eh?'

'No sir.'

'What's it like, sir?' John asked.

'Like? The main part is built of stone. Has a fine view. It stands on a hill above the beach, and there is a small pier. Some of the boys have their own sailing boats. They make them.'

'How many boys are there?' Jason asked.

'Oh, I couldn't say, but they must be pretty well full up for boys go there from all over the West Indies. There are not many boarding schools for white boys in the islands, you know. And there will be evacuees like yourselves, and boys who would normally go back to England, or to the States to school. Yes, they'll be pretty well full up.' He looked at Jason's gloomy face. 'Think you'll like it?' he asked.

'I'm sure it will be all right,' John hastened to say. 'Only it's hard to start a new school just as you've got used to one. But I don't mind.'

'I love going to new places,' Andrew assured everyone, his spectacles gleaming.

Across the water came the boom of the loud speaker. 'Will Mr Nobbs please go at once to the Purser's office. I beg your pardon, I should have said Miss Nobbs. Miss Nobbs, to the Purser's office please. Passengers are asked to look on the bath lists to see where their names occur, and not to ask for baths out of their turns.'

'We came on that ship from Liverpool,' Andrew said. 'But we like this one better,' he added hastily. 'You haven't a loud speaker, have you, sir?'

'No,' said the Captain. 'No, we scarcely need it here.'

'I like a small ship,' Andrew said loyally. 'You're nearer to the water, and it is isn't so much like a hotel.'

'Less like it than before the war,' the Captain said with his eyes twinkling. 'Shine your own shoes, and no early morning cup of tea, at least for passengers, eh, Dix?'

'When are we going?' Andrew asked.

The Captain regarded him quizzically. 'The rule is,' he said, 'that I may ask you questions, but you can't ask me any.'

'There's a war on, Monkey,' John said.

Jason muttered, 'Little stupe!'

'Oh, I didn't mean that!' Andrew said, flushing bright red. 'I didn't mean anything like that, really I didn't. I didn't mean anything except that I wondered whether there would be time for me to go and get some chocolate from the automatic machine at the end of the wharf.'

'Better ask the guard at the head of the gangway,' the Captain said. 'They wouldn't let you go far. And you can't leave the wharf without a landing permit. But what I came to ask you to do for me is this: I want you to gather all the children on board together at four o'clock in my cabin.'

'Up on the bridge, sir?' Andrew piped, recovering himself.

'Yes. And, Jason, as you're the eldest, see that no one is left out. There are about nineteen, I believe, including babies. See to it, will you? Tell the mothers. In about...' he looked at his watch. 'In about an hour's time.' He waved his hand, and strode off with his friend.

'What do you suppose he wants us for?' Andrew demanded when he was out of sight.

'You cut along and find all the children, and tell them or their mothers about it,' Jason said. 'And just make a list of the ones you tell, and bring it back to me when you've finished.'

'We'll have to make Pat go,' Andrew said. 'He's still standing behind the door in the cabin.' He took out a large black note-book from his pocket. 'I'll just put the names down in here,' he said. 'I'll begin with us three.'

'Look, Monkey, there's a lady waving at you,' John said. Jason, who had been fingering his tie with a self-conscious air immediately stopped, and fixed a savage eye on a broken box that was floating in the dock. There certainly was a lady, very young and smart in her American Red Cross uniform, waving towards them from the top of the gangway.

'It's my friend,' Andrew piped. He raced to the corner of the deck nearest her, and waved frantically. She descended the gangway to the dock in company with a young American officer, and before disappearing into the goods shed, she blew a kiss to Andrew, who shamelessly returned it. He came back grinning from ear to ear.

'Wasn't she simply smashing!' he exclaimed with a happy sigh. The other boys remained silent. Jason still gloomily regarded the box below. John whistled under his breath. Andrew went on, not deceived by their apparent lack of interest. 'She's the lady who took Pat and me out this morning,' he said. 'She had a special permit. We went to the Empire State building, and to Radio City, and then we had a walnut double - cream - strawberry - chocolate - ice-cream sundae. Oh boy!' He smacked his lips. 'We had quite a long talk,' Andrew said dreamily, though his companions made no comment. 'We had a long talk. You know sometimes you feel as if you had known a person for a long time.'

'Is there anyone you can't feel that way about?' John asked.

'Well, anyhow, she's simply smashing. She asked where we were going to, and I told her all about us.'

'You what?'

Jason grabbed Andrew by the scruff of the neck and pretended to lift him up preparatory to dropping him over the rail.

'Just what did you tell her about us?' he asked.

'Nothing. Everything. Ouch! let go! Just about what schools we were at when war broke out, and how we met at Liverpool and all that.'

'Kindly tell me what you told her about me!' Jason demanded, giving him a shake.

'Ow! Jason, stop it! I just told her that you were the

champion boxer of your prep school and that you hated being evacuated, and that your father was in the Navy, and that we were all going to Badanda College.'

'And what did you discourse about me?' John said affably, but laying a menacing hand upon his wrist.

'Well, I told her that you were awfully fond of sweets, and could make cakes, and that you could play the piano awfully well. And that you were both jolly decent fellows. Ouch!' he added, as Jason and John both tightened their hold upon him.

'The next time anyone wants to have a long, interesting conversation with you, Monkey,' Jason said in ominous, though cracked tones, 'you don't know anything about *us*, do you understand?'

'Like your cheek, discussing us with a perfect stranger,' John said.

Andrew gave a sniff of injured innocence.

'I don't know why you are making all this fuss, and spoiling my clean collar,' he said. 'I was only showing what good fellows you were.'

'Well, I'm warning you not to do it again, that's all,' Jason said. 'And if you say one word more about me and what I can or can't do, or what I feel about anything, I'll drop you over the side where there are plenty of sharks.'

'I don't care,' Andrew said. 'Sharks don't bite. I read that somewhere in a book of nature stories. It said it was a common mistake.'

'Well, we'll test it, won't we?' Jason asked John.

'No use, Jass old son,' John said solemnly. 'I know for a fact that sharks don't eat skinny monkeys.'

'Of course I told her all about my stamp collection, and how it got left behind in my school,' Andrew went on. 'And about Pat being good at puzzles.'

'In fact, you revealed everything, it seems,' Jason said. 'Well next time leave me out of your confidences, please.'

'And me!' John added.

'And now get on with it,' Jason ordered. 'Find the children and marshal them all at the door of the captain's cabin by four o'clock. You won't have much time to spare.'

'I say, Jason,' Andrew grinned, poised just beyond arm's reach, 'you asked me to try going on to the bridge, didn't you? Ha! ha! you never thought we'd get an invitation up there.' He dashed off, his ears and notebook waving.

'*Our friends of the American Red Cross have sent a box of presents for you*'

'What do you suppose the skipper wants us for?' Jason asked, turning back to the rail.

'I suppose he wants to warn us not to let go of our life-belts or something,' John said,

'Rats! He wouldn't want the babies up to tell them that!'

'Well, don't worry. We'll know soon enough,' John said lazily.

'I hope he's not going to give a lot of pi-jaw. I was fed up being ordered about by numbers on the other ship,' Jason said unexpectedly.

'I didn't think you minded.'

'Well, I did,' Jason said shortly, his voice breaking. 'And that's why I'm glad there's no loud speaker on this ship.'

But whatever their guesses were as to the Captain's reasons for inviting them to visit him, they were all surprised to see an enormous box on the deck outside his door. In the cabin the table was covered with bags.

'Well,' the Captain said when all of them were crowded into his quarters. 'I suppose you want to know what I asked you all up here for, eh? The fact is, that our friends of the American Red Cross have sent a box of presents for you, and we'll just begin by passing out these.' To each he presented a bag of sweets. Then from the box outside the door he began to unpack parcels, reading the name on each and handing it to the right person with the aid of Andrew, who had constituted himself his helper. The babies received rattles or soft toys; the little girls dolls and books. For Pat who had obediently accompanied Jason and John, there was a box of construction toys. Andrew whistled with delight over a stamp album. John was presented with a book of music, and Jason with a pair of boxing gloves. The party did not take long, and soon the children were streaming down from the bridge with their treasures. Pat immediately returned to the cabin, sat on the floor, and began to examine his set. Jean and Guy went to show their gifts to their mother, accompanied by Andrew. In Cabin 58 John said,

'Let's see the gloves, Jason. Not bad, eh? Put them on.'

Jason did so. The expression on his face was not easy to read. He looked as though he were trying hard not to feel pleased.

'They're good enough gloves,' he said, making a reluctant feint or two. 'Only ...'

'What's the matter?'

'Only ... I felt rotten at first when the Captain gave them to me ... As if we were refugees ...'

'Well, I suppose we are,' John said. 'Evacuees ... Refugees ... What's the difference? We're here, aren't we? Any old how, you'll be able to use them at Badanda College.'

'What did you get, John?'

'A book of piano duets,' John answered. 'Awfully nice, of course, but not much use unless I can get someone to play them with me.'

That evening the cabin steward came round to insert into the portholes the metal disks that made them light-proof. Pat pointed out this to Mrs Grant when she came to see that the two younger boys were in bed for the night. Her own two children were asleep, and Andrew could be heard singing in his bath where, presumably, he was learning to float.

'They've blacked out the portholes. That means we'll start before morning,' Pat said.

'Do you think so, Pat?'

'Yes. There are no lights on deck, either.'

'Well, go to sleep, Pat, and if you want anything, call me.'

It was close on midnight when the whistle of a launch awoke Mrs Grant. She was aware then of the throbbing of the ship's engines. She got up softly, put on her dressing-gown, and pushed past the canvas curtains that separated the corridor from the well deck. Two tugs had entered the dock basin, and were getting into position to pull the ship out into the river. The gangways had already been removed, and men stood ready to cast off the mooring ropes. Mrs Grant went to the side to watch. Gradually the space between the ship's side and the wharf widened, and soon the wind of the open river was blowing freshly across the deck. The lights of New York and Brooklyn, and the moving lights of traffic along the shore, the red and green lights of the ships, and the far-off glinting of the stars were reflected in the blackness of the river. Somewhere ahead was the meeting place of the ships for the convoy. Once out of port, the stars would be the only lights they would see until they reached Tripadoes. It was the start of the second lap of their journey to Badanda College. Lost in these thoughts, Mrs Grant was surprised at last to find that it was nearly two o'clock in the morning.

She went back to her cabin, but before entering, she noticed that the door of 58 was ajar. She went and looked in. All was dark and quiet. Too quiet. There was not even the sound of breathing. She turned the lights on, and found all the bunks empty.

'They've gone on deck to watch,' she said to herself. For a moment she stood undecided. If the boys had all been as old as Jason or John she might have left them to return by themselves; but she felt uneasy about Andrew and Pat.

Finally, after waiting in her cabin for about an hour without hearing them return, she dressed, and went up to search the lounge and smoking-room. They were empty. The doors leading to the upper deck were closed, and the entrances masked with indirect passages and canvas curtains. Once in the open, Mrs Grant had to wait for a moment or two before she could get used to the gloom. Then she made out the forms of people by the rails, and decided that almost all the passengers must be on deck. Groping her way along, she made a complete circuit of the upper deck. It was like a game of blindman's-buff, for she had to feel each person to decide whether he was small enough to be one of the boys. This caused some natural surprise, and she had to explain what she was doing. At the end of the deck she saw a person standing by himself who looked tall enough to be Jason. She put her hand up to his shoulder, and as the man turned at that moment she found herself stroking a silky, bearded face.

'I beg your pardon,' she said. 'But I am looking for some boys who are in my care. They have gone from their cabin. Have you seen them?'

'I think I saw a couple of boys going towards the gunners' deck in the stern,' a pleasant voice said. 'As like as not they will be there. Allow me to come and help you. My name is Dix.'

Mrs Grant thanked him, and they climbed down to the well deck. It was not easy to find their way across between the hatches, the winches, and the enormous cases which had been lashed between the spars, but at last they reached the ladder leading to the gunners' turret. Mrs Grant was relieved to hear the sound of voices. Jason and John were there talking to the men on watch.

'Where are Andrew and Pat?' she asked.

'They were in bed when we came on deck,' John said.

'Well, they are not there now. In this black-out they might fall into a hatch or over the side, and no one would see them.'

'We'll come and help you look for them,' John said.

'I wish you would. I've been all over the inside of the ship.'

'Have you looked in the crew's quarters, or the galley?' Mr Dix asked.

'No,' Mrs Grant answered.

'Well, suppose we divide up,' Dix suggested. 'I can't see either of you boys in this darkness, but I'll go with this one.' His hand groped and grasped John's arm. 'We'll look everywhere below. The other boy had better go with you, Mrs ... er ...'

'Grant.'

'Thank you. This is a queer introduction, isn't it? These two, if I am not mistaken, I met this afternoon. Well, is this agreed?'

'Thank you, yes.'

Jason and Mrs Grant groped back again across the well deck.

'Have you been up at the bows?' Jason asked.

'No. Could they go up there?'

'Oh, yes; they let us go anywhere, almost.'

'Let's go, then.' They made their way the length of the ship and climbed to the bows. Andrew's cheerful laugh was borne back to them on the wind. He was talking with great animation to the look-out man, in the pitch darkness.

But of Pat there was no sign.

CHAPTER 2

A Search in the Black-out

'BUT where is Pat?' Mrs Grant asked.

'I don't know,' Andrew replied. 'He's somewhere about, I suppose, if he's not in bed. He was asleep when I came up.'

'Well, he's not there now. The cabin's empty.'

'Did you look behind the door?'

'No, I didn't.'

'He may be there,' Andrew declared cheerfully. 'Or he may be under the bunk or in the cupboard. He's like that. The engines and whistles woke me. I saw that John and Jason were up, and thought I'd have a look too. Isn't it simply smashing to see the lights in the river! Do you think that high building over there is the Empire State? Do you suppose we'll be in convoy in the morning? What do . . .'

'Andrew!' Mrs Grant said impatiently, 'we must find Pat. Come and help us. Until we find him we don't want to do anything else.'

'Righto!' Andrew said. 'Let me go first, because I'm used to this deck, and it's full of chains. It's dark, isn't it? I'll help you.' He extended a friendly hand, and guided Mrs Grant down the companionway and across the well deck.

But Pat was not behind the door, nor under the bunk, nor in the galley, nor in any other part of the ship that they could think of. John and Dix came back to report no success.

'We've found Andrew,' Mrs Grant said, 'but not Pat Duncan.'

'Pat Duncan?' Dix echoed, in an odd tone.

'Yes, he's the youngest of the four,' Mrs Grant said. 'That's why I'm so anxious.'

'We used to play a game called sardines,' Andrew said blithely. 'One person hides and the others go and hide with him as they find him. Only we haven't found him.' He seemed to have no fears as to the fate of his companion.

'Now that we've done all we can, I suppose we must report him missing,' Mrs Grant said, in great distress. 'Where can he be?'

'He'll be all right, I think,' Jason said. 'He's a stolid sort of child, and I don't think he's likely to get into danger.' He looked at his bunk as if he contemplated turning in.

Mrs Grant flushed.

'You don't seem to understand,' she said, 'that a small boy, only eight years old, is missing. He may have fallen overboard, or down a hatch. You're the oldest, and should feel some responsibility for him.'

'He was asleep when we left the cabin,' Jason said stiffly.

'You might have known that he would wake up.'

Jason said nothing. He stared over her head at the wall.

'Well,' Mrs Grant said finally, 'we must report it . . .'

'Allow me to go with you,' Dix said. 'I think one of us should stay here and wait in case he comes back.'

'Will you do that, Jason?' Mrs Grant asked.

'All right.' Jason sat down on the bunk assuming a lack of interest which he did not really feel. He had been told off, not only in the presence of his friends, but of this man Dix to whom Andrew had already given the name of Goldbeard.

Not noticing Jason's resentment, Mrs Grant followed Dix as he enlisted the aid of the Officer in charge. But no one had seen Pat. He was not in the laundry where the Chinese laundrymen were gambling. He was not with the apprentices in the fo'c'sle, nor in the engine rooms, nor in the pantries, nor in the baggage rooms. He had not strayed by mistake into the cabin of another passenger. John prowled along, searching dark corridors. Andrew crawled in an agile, spiderish fashion under all the settees in the smoking-room, and even opened the grand piano to peep into it.

'Do you think,' Mrs Grant asked, 'that he would have climbed the rigging?'

'Never!' Andrew assured her. 'He's too frightened to do anything really dangerous.'

'Where can he be, then?' Mrs Grant murmured. She was as much alarmed by the anxious silence of Dix as by the conjectures of the boys. The only good thing was that dawn was beginning to break, and the search would no longer have to be carried on in complete darkness on deck. In one of her trips down to the cabin to see if Pat had returned, Mrs Grant heard Jean calling her from number 60.

'What's the matter, mummie?' Jean asked as her mother came in. 'Why are you dressed? Is it time to get up?'

'No, dear. We are looking for Pat.'

'What's happened to him?'

'We don't know. He's not in his cabin.'

'I expect he's hiding,' Jean said. 'We found an awfully good place to hide this afternoon. Perhaps he's there.' She chuckled sleepily.

'Oh Jean, where?'

'Up on deck.'

'Put on your dressing-gown, darling, and come and show us.'

Jean was delighted to get up at such an unusual hour. With a desperate hope the others followed her. There were two doors from the smoking-room on to the deck. They were both veiled by indirect approaches covered with canvas curtains so that no light would show; but on the starboard side the door was locked and the passage-way covered by the canvas was really a blind alley. At the end of this, huddled in his coat, they found Pat, fast asleep.

CHAPTER 3

Straws Show Which Way the Wind Blows

THE relief was so great that Mrs Grant said very little. She thanked Dix for his kindness, and she looked so tired that he suggested that she go down at once to her cabin to get the rest which she had lost during the night.

'I'll stay with the youngsters,' he said. Jean and Andrew had forgotten Pat's escapade at once in the excitement of seeing the convoy formed. They begged to be allowed to stay on deck and watch instead of going back to bed. Mrs Grant gave in, and left them on deck.

Jason said nothing, even to John, but at the time when she had reproved him in the presence of the others, Jason had vowed never to speak to her unless he had to. From that hour, whenever she appeared he put on an impassive face, and when a direct question needed an answer, gave it with icy civility. He would not even smile in her presence, and always withdrew from a group if she joined it. John saw it all, but even his friendship for Jason would not persuade him to act in the same way.

It happened that the day after leaving port Mrs Grant appeared in the door of Cabin 58 to see that all was tidy for the Captain's inspection. John's new book of piano duets was lying on his bunk, and Mrs Grant asked,

'May I look at your music?'

'Certainly,' John answered, handing it to her.

Jason left the cabin with rather too much dignity.

'This is a nice collection,' Mrs Grant said. 'Will you let me try them with you?'

'I'd like to very much,' John replied pleasantly.

'Well, suppose we say eleven o'clock in the morning when Guy is taking his rest? I think the smoking-room is fairly empty at that hour.'

'I'd like to, thank you,' John said, though he did not look

forward particularly to playing duets with her. He had often had to play with people who were not good enough to make it interesting for him, and it was very boring. He did not know anything about Mrs Grant's playing. At eleven o'clock when he and Jason were playing chess in the smoking-room she appeared. When she saw how the boys were occupied she hesitated, but John rose.

'I don't want to disturb you at your game,' she demurred.

'That's all right,' John said. 'We were only killing time.'

She glanced at Jason who sat brooding over the pieces as if he had not heard the conversation. John went to the piano, opened it, arranged the music and the chairs, and smilingly waited for Mrs Grant to take her place. When they had started Jason got up and went out on deck. It did not take John long to realize that Mrs Grant could play as well as he did. Time flew by, and they were both surprised when they heard the luncheon gong banged in a peculiar rhythm.

'Good gracious!' Mrs Grant said, rising hastily, 'I had no idea it was so late. Guy will be awake. Thank you so much! I have enjoyed it. John, you play well.'

'So do you,' John smiled.

'But,' Mrs Grant said frankly, 'I will never play any better than I do now, and you will. I won't be in your class in another two years.'

'It's very kind of you to say so,' John said.

'I hope you'll let me play with you again,' Mrs Grant said. 'This is the only time of day we can do it. No one seems to have been disturbed by us. Good gracious, what a din!'

The smoking-room door was flung open and Andrew appeared beating the gong to the rhythm of 'John Brown's body.' Mrs Grant fled.

'Give that here, you glorious lunatic,' John said, collaring Andrew.

'But the dining-room steward said I could!' Andrew protested. 'Ouch, John, you fathead, let me go!' Impudently he gave John a poke with the stick and the next instant they were scuffling on the floor, while the gong went rolling along the corridor.

'What's all this?' an agreeable tenor voice asked. There stood Mr Dix, smiling. The gong, having reached the end of the hall, now fell down with a loud clang.

'The steward said I could bang the gong!' Andrew shouted, struggling with John for the stick.

'So you were responsible for that burst of sound, Little Friend of All the World,' Goldbeard said. John let go of the

Andrew ran by banging the gong

stick, and Andrew fell over backwards. Without waiting to get to his feet he scrambled between the tall man's legs, and picking up the gong, fled, slamming the door behind him. A victorious banging announced his arrival on deck.

'Great lad that!' Dix laughed. 'By the way, I enjoyed your music just now.'

'Thanks, sir.'

'You must play in the concert,' Dix said. 'See you later, at lunch.' He waved his hand and vanished in the direction of the bridge.

When John went to get ready for lunch he found that Jason, instead of waiting for him as usual, had gone in by himself. Most of the tables in the dining saloon were small ones. Mrs Grant had arranged to take Pat and Andrew with her two children at one table, leaving the older two free to sit where they chose. The steward found them places on the other side with two men, Mr Johnstone and Mr Dix. The former was an old Scotsman and very deaf. He was the manager of a sugar estate to which he was returning. He was always the first at table, and the first to leave. Mr Dix, on the other hand, seldom appeared until the meal was half over.

John found that Jason and Mr Johnstone had started their meal.

'Why didn't you wait for me?' he said in a tone of cheerful remonstrance. Jason scowled. John ordered soup. Then he noticed Jason's expression. 'What's the matter?' he asked.

Their deaf table companion went on with his meal without paying any attention to them. Jason still said nothing.

'It's no use your being angry with me,' John said affably, 'because I'm going to be your pal through thick and thin.' He grinned disarmingly. 'Come on, Jass old son, loosen up!'

'You don't need to put yourself out to befriend me,' Jason said coldly.

'Oh, come off it!'

'What would you think if I left you and went off in the middle of a game?'

'How could I help it, when Dame Grant said that that was the only time she had? I warned you when we started.'

'You could have said that you were doing something else.'

'Don't be a chump. We've got to be polite to her. Besides,' John added calmly, 'she plays jolly well.'

'All right! All right! Play duets with her as much as you like, but don't expect me to hang about for you!'

'Oh, dry up! I think you're a stupe! Anyhow, it was decent of her to take those two infants off our hands at meals.'

B

'What she does is not of the slightest interest to me,' Jason said.

'You gump! You stiff-necked gump!' exclaimed John. 'Still,' he added with his usual good nature as he finished his soup, 'it's no use, Jass old son. It takes two to make a quarrel, and I'm not going to be in this one. Dear old pal!' he said in a melodramatic undertone.

This flippancy was too much for Jason. He muttered something savage under his breath. Their deaf companion, having reached the end of his meal, rose, put in his chair, and with a nod of acknowledgement, left the table. Almost at the same time Goldbeard Dix slid into his chair.

'Well, well! Late as usual, eh?' he laughed with a flash of white teeth. 'What's on the card to-day? Anything nice? Hm ... curried shrimps, waiter,' he said in an aside. 'I've just found out that the Chief Engineer has a punching bag. He's going to put it up on the well deck this afternoon. Either of you boys box?'

'Jason does,' John said.

'We're going to arrange for a few exhibition rounds,' Dix said in his resonant tenor voice. 'Do you suppose the good lady in charge of you would mind if you put your fists up? Perhaps you'd better ask her.'

This reference to Mrs Grant instantly made Jason decide to enter the contest.

'I'll do what I can,' he said in his usual voice. He did not care to advertise his quarrel to the outside world. 'But I'm too light,' he added.

'Some of the apprentices are about your size,' Dix said, appraising Jason's torso with critical eyes. 'We thought of arranging a show for the ship's charity fund.'

'If I could get some practice,' said Jason, 'I wouldn't mind.'

It thus came about that while Mrs Grant and John played duets Jason went and sparred with the apprentices. There was plenty for everyone to do, for the ship was crowded. In ordinary times the little freighter might carry thirty passengers. Now there were over ninety. There were few comforts, but no one grumbled. There were a number of elderly people on board, many of whom had come out of retirement to resume work. There were officials going to the West Indies, and some men going to join the Services at the Military and Naval bases. There were a few South American passengers who were hoping to continue from Tripadoes in sloops or inter-island steamers. For the first few days they seemed a confused crowd, and then suddenly everyone knew the names of all the others. Being in convoy made the trip different from ordinary voyages. Day after day they woke to find themselves in their line, with the same ships in the same places spaced like pieces on a gigantic chess board: tankers, freighters, liners, aircraft, all obeying the orders of the commodore, and being shepherded by the corvettes which were on ceaseless patrol on the horizon. And every day airplanes from bases in the Caribbean flew overhead to mark their progress.

Mr Dix was the natural leader of the passengers, both by temperament and ability. Andrew worshipped him and pursued him relentlessly.

'I must see Goldbeard first thing,' he said one morning. He was the first one up, and was dressing.

'Oh, give him a rest!' Jason ordered.

'But he likes me. I'm his friend.'

'You'll make an enemy of him if you bother him all the time.'

'That's where you're wrong,' Andrew said with importance. 'I write notes of interesting things to tell him, in my notebook, and every morning we sit down and read out the items.'

John reached from his bunk and grabbed Andrew.

'Give it here,' he commanded.

'Ouch, John, you're pinching me!'

'Give it here, I say.'

'Give what, fathead?'

'That notebook,' John said.

'But it's my private notebook.'

'Has it got things about us in it?'

'Yes, but . . .'

'Hand it over!'

'I won't!'

Jason leant down from his upper bunk and picked Andrew up by the scruff of the neck.

'I'll hold him while you search him,' he said.

John had no difficulty in finding the notebook, as it was as big as a small dictionary.

'Here we are,' he said.

'Oh give it back to me, you brutish beast!' Andrew piped plaintively. 'It's private!'

'Of course a beast is brutish,' John said genially, turning over the leaves of the book. 'It would be as sensible to say "you human man!"'

As Andrew still kicked rebelliously, Jason hauled him up and made him sit on the edge of the upper bunk.

'Just scrutinize the book, will you?' he said, 'while I keep the author under restraint.' John flicked over the leaves.

'It seems to be lists of food mostly,' he said, 'and bath times. Oh yes, here we are. . . . Hm . . .'

'Read it out loud,' Jason commanded, while Andrew wailed and besought them to give him back his book.

'So I'm fat and lazy, am I?' John said. 'Not so lazy but that I'll give you a good walloping when I get up, young fellow-me-lad.'

'Read it!' Jason insisted.

'Modesty forbids, almost,' John said. 'I wish you'd learn to spell, Andrew. How do you expect me to understand what you write when you make so many mistakes?'

'I don't want you to read it at all,' said Andrew. 'I know perfectly well what I have written.'

' "Jason is the eldest, and the bigest," ' John read out. ' "He thinks he is very dignerfied, but when he is angery his voice brakes. He has to elder brothers and wants to go into the navvy. He boxes and is going to Badanda. I forget the name of his last shool." He's got your name, age, and address in England,' John added.

'Is that all about me?' Jason demanded.

'That's all on this page. What does it mean when a paragraph has a tick against it?' he asked Andrew.

'That means that I've read it to Goldbeard,' Andrew chirped.

'You miserable little worm! Well, it seems that all four of our names and addresses and little bits of information are down here. "Mr Brown is a diver, and is going to do some speashul work in ..." I don't know what this word is. How do you know he's a diver?'

''Cause I saw his diving suit in his cabin, and asked him.'

'You would. Here's some more about us: "Pat is some speashul kind of infant. Prodigal son or progeny. It means he is cleaver at things more than moast pepul. He is the only one in his family, and I think his mother must be dead because he can't remember her." ' John stopped abruptly, glancing at Pat, who was solemnly pulling on his stockings, paying no attention to the others.

'What bally right have you to write all these things down?' Jason asked, giving Andrew a shake.

'Why shouldn't I? Goldbeard says I have a literal turn of mind.'

'I suppose you mean "literary".'

'It means that perhaps I'll write books when I grow up.'

'If you live to grow up!' Jason said ominously.

'Everything that you have written so far has been ticked; so that means that you've reported them all, does it?'

'Yes. I'm going to write some more after breakfast.'

'Not about us, you're not!' Jason said. 'We've warned you before not to discuss our private affairs with strangers.'

'How are you going to keep me from writing, fathead?'

'Just tear out those pages about us, will you, John?' Jason asked. 'And if we ever find any more, you will be for it, young nuisance!' John added his threats of vengeance to those of Jason, and Andrew was allowed to depart. He was not at all abashed.

'I can't think why Mr Dix wants to bother with all that

tosh,' Jason said thoughtfully. 'He's a decent sort, and a jolly good boxer. Have you seen him with the punching bag?'

'Yes. And he has some good records. What do you think, Jason! He's got a wireless fixed up in his cabin.'

'How's that?'

'I don't know. It's against the rules. He asked me if I'd like to hear a concert from New York, after dinner some night. I said of course I would.'

'I don't suppose anyone would mind that,' Jason said doubtfully. It was impossible not to excuse Goldbeard. He was certainly the most popular passenger.

Mrs Grant found him charming. He would play with Guy and Jean and seemed to enjoy himself thoroughly in their company. As they went southwards and the blacked-out ship grew hotter Mrs Grant used to spend many of the hours of darkness up on deck, unable to sleep in the airless cabin. She frequently met Goldbeard there and found him a most interesting talker. It seemed that he had tried his hand at many things, and owned in Tripadoes a motor car business. He also had motor boats. 'But of course in war time most of my cars and boats have been commandeered,' he said.

In turn she told him more perhaps than she intended. Her husband was at sea somewhere, and the thought of his danger was never out of her mind. She had accepted the post at Badanda both as a means of getting the children out of war-time England, and occupying herself. She found herself talking to Goldbeard about the boys. Jason seemed sullen, and she was doubtful about his influence with the others.

'I shouldn't worry too much about him,' Dix said comfortingly. 'Jason's a very normal sort of lad. He is at a sensitive age. Pretend not to notice, and he'll grow out of it.'

'John's much easier to deal with,' Mrs Grant continued. 'And we have music in common. He is really talented.'

'As for Andrew,' Dix said, with a hearty laugh, 'He is everybody's friend.'

'Oh yes. I never have trouble with him. I hope he does not bother you.'

'Not a bit. He's a bit of a contrast to the other small one, isn't he?'

Mrs Grant made some reply which brushed the question aside. She could not have told why she did not care to discuss Pat with Goldbeard. He was to her the most interesting and perplexing child of the four. He seemed to live in a world of his own, and it certainly was not stupidity that kept him silent.

She thought of this next day as she sat with Pat and Jean and Guy on deck. As the weather grew warmer, and the lounge was almost unbearably hot, most of the passengers spent all the time they could outside, sitting on their rugs and coats in the absence of deck-chairs. Andrew went around telling people not to sit on their life-jackets.

'Why not, Andrew?' Jean asked rebelliously, looking up from the cat she was drawing.

'Because the Chief Officer said we weren't to.'

'That's not a reason,' Jean said. 'Why not, Pat?'

'Because the kapok stuffing will get pressed hard, and wouldn't float so well.'

'Pat knows everything,' Jean said with satisfaction. 'What's that thick cable thing here by the rail, Pat?'

'It's the degaussing cable,' said Pat.

'What does it do?'

'If the ship goes over a magnetic mine it won't explode.'

'Bravo, Pat!' said a tenor voice. There was Mr Dix, looking larger and more brilliant than ever because he had changed into white tropical clothes. Jean instantly demanded that Goldbeard should sit down and draw for her.

'Perhaps Mr Dix has something else to do,' Mrs Grant said.

'I have half an hour to spare,' he said cheerfully. 'In the meanwhile Andrew will run at full speed all round the ship and get the names of those who want to enter the deck tennis tournament. Shall we start with yours, Mrs Grant?'

'I'm afraid I can't leave Guy,' she said.

'Nonsense! Guy will sit with me in the umpire's chair

while you are playing, eh, Guy? Put her name down, Andrew.'

'Oky doke!' Andrew said, licking his pencil and writing busily.

'Now off you go, Andy old man,' Mr Dix said heartily. 'Get all the names. Tell the fat ones that the exercise will reduce them, and the thin ones that they will be sure to win.'

'Righto!' shrilled Andrew, dashing off at full speed.

'That'll keep him for half an hour anyway,' chuckled Goldbeard. 'Now what are we doing here? Colouring pictures, eh? Who drew this?'

'Pat did,' Jean said, putting scribbles of red all over the ship which Pat had drawn.

'Fine! Fine!' he said. 'Will you draw me a picture, Pat?'

'I've finished drawing,' Pat said.

'Well, I'll draw you one, Jean,' Goldbeard said. 'By the way, Mrs Grant, we're getting up a ship's concert. You will play, won't you?'

'I might do a duet with John,' Mrs Grant said. 'Or play a few accompaniments for you.'

'Splendid. I'll put you down. Wish we could have it on deck. It's getting far too hot in the evening inside, especially with the black-out and not a port open. Sacrifice ourselves for a good cause, eh? And then there's the boxing contest. You don't mind if young Jason enters, do you?'

'I don't know much about boxing,' she said rather fearfully. 'Are you sure he won't get hurt?'

'No, not a bit of it. He'll only be up against the young apprentices who are about his own weight.' Dix suddenly picked up a sketch of an aeroplane. 'Whose is this?' he asked.

'It's mine,' Jean said. 'Pat did it for me.'

'Will you give it to me, Jean?'

'Yes, I will,' Jean said in an adoring voice.

'Thank you, Jean. And will you sign it for me?' Goldbeard went on with an engaging smile. 'All great artists sign their work, don't they, Mrs Grant?' He held it out to Pat.

'No,' said the child.

'Why not, Pat?' asked Mrs Grant, but the little boy did not answer. His was the only silent voice in the chorus of admiration about Goldbeard. There was a moment of embarrassment.

'Look, there's Andrew coming,' Jean sang out.

'Help!' Goldbeard whispered in mock trepidation. 'Let me escape! Hush!' He went down on all fours and scuttled crabwise around the corner of the deck, giving an amusing grimace as he vanished. Andrew came up panting.

'Got all the names,' he said, 'but where is Goldbeard?'

'He's run away from you,' Jean chuckled. For a moment Andrew seemed disconcerted, but he soon recovered.

'I'll find him when he goes to boxing at eleven,' he said.

'I'm glad to see you helpful, Andrew,' Mrs Grant said, 'but you don't want to worry people, you know.'

'I don't worry people,' Andrew exclaimed, really surprised.

'Of course not,' Mrs Grant said hastily. 'Only . . .'

'Goldbeard likes me to be with him,' Andrew said earnestly. 'I tell him all the news. I found out about what people can do for the concert, and everything.'

'Mr Goldbeard took one of Pat's drawings,' Jean said. 'But Pat wouldn't write his name on it.'

'Why not, fathead?'

Pat said nothing.

'He didn't want to,' Jean said. 'He didn't have to if he didn't want to, did he? And he's not a fathead.'

'Gently, children!' Mrs Grant remonstrated.

'I told Goldbeard that Pat was a prodigious infant,' Andrew remarked.

'What do you mean, Andrew?' Mrs Grant demanded.

'Well, you know how musicians play the piano and make up pieces and things when they are about four years old?'

'Oh, you mean infant prodigies.'

'Yes, that's what he called it. I said that, didn't I? Prodigious infants. He's that sort of an infant about machines and puzzles and so on. Of course he ought to be, because his father is Kelmscott Montford-Duncan, the celebrated scientist and inventor. Isn't he, young Pat?' Pat said nothing. He was staring at the sea with an expression that baffled Mrs Grant. 'I told him that Pat's second name was Kelmscott. I saw it on his passport. And he said it was the name of the famous engine designer.'

Mrs Grant stared at Pat. Against his name on the paper she had received was an address of a guardian in England. Andrew's declaration touched some chord of memory in her mind, but she was roused from her meditation by the sound of the boat drill alarm. They were all used to it by now, and lost no time in taking their places with their life jackets adjusted. Jason was annoyed, having been summoned from a sparring practice. John strolled up good-naturedly with a book, which he continued to read after he had taken his stand. Andrew hopped about trying the little red lights attached to the shoulders of the jackets.

'Yours won't go on, Mrs Grant,' he said excitedly. 'Pat, can you fix this? Let me tell the First Officer that it won't work.'

He rushed off at full speed, and was caught and sent back by Dix.

'Now, young Andrew,' Goldbeard cried. 'Orders must be obeyed, eh? Back you go.' His blue eyes swept the line, and lingered on Pat. He helped Mrs Grant to adjust the harness which was especially made for tiny children. Jean and Guy were always restless at having to wait for the officer to inspect. They ran round and round their mother, tugging at her skirts. Goldbeard picked Guy up, letting the child ride on his shoulder. Pat stood quietly in his place. He had tested his red light, and found it working. He stared out at the sea. On either hand as far as the horizon ships kept in line with them. Ahead and behind stood ships, all keeping their places as if they stood still.

'It's like being in a sea-city,' Andrew said. 'There are water streets, and the Commodore's ship is the Town Hall. And those little corvettes whizzing round outside and riding up and down between the lines of ships are policemen telling us all to move on and keep in our lines. If any ship doesn't obey orders it will be taken prisoner.'

They all took their places at the sound of the boat drill alarm

Jean began to laugh delightedly as Andrew embroidered his theme. Her mother did not hear her. She was staring at Pat. The word had given her memory a jolt. A prisoner. Kelmscott Montford-Duncan! She remembered now having read about him in a recent paper. The famous inventor had been attending a conference in Germany when the war broke out, and he had been detained. He was a prisoner of war, and this was his son.

A strange lurch of the ship threw them all out of line.

'What's that?' Jason asked.

'Something's wrong,' John said, steadying himself against the rail.

'We must be changing course, I suppose,' Andrew shouted.

'Steering gear's gone wrong,' Pat said quietly.

Goldbeard Dix took a few steps forward. 'But we'll be late,' he said as if involuntarily. He had taken his hand from Guy, and the little boy almost fell from his shoulder. Mrs Grant sprang forward and caught him. Dix's face was strangely agitated. He looked at her as if he saw only something in his own thoughts. Mrs Grant took Jean by the hand, and ordered the boys to stay close, and not to move away from their places. Plainly something was wrong. The ship veered from her course and went blundering sideways through the lines of the convoy. The passengers huddled against the rail, trying to see what was amiss, and uncertain what to do. Officers and crew started to run to their stations. A black board was being hoisted up to the masthead, and the ship continued its helpless drift, with all the other vessels scrambling out of her way. A corvette now came racing alongside. The commodore's signal was going madly.

'We weren't struck by anything, were we?' Mrs Grant asked. Dix seemed to recall where he was.

'I . . . I didn't hear anything,' he said. 'Here's the Second Officer. I'll ask him.'

'It's the steering gear,' the officer said. 'They're working on it. No, I don't know how long it will be.' He was gone.

Through the lines of ships they blundered on, until they reached the outermost edge of the convoy, and saw the rest sailing on without them.

'They won't leave us all alone, will they?' Mrs Grant asked with trembling lips.

'They may reduce speed,' Goldbeard said in a voice unlike his usual confident one. 'It's not likely that they will stop.'

'But they've forgotten all about the life-boat drill,' Andrew piped up.

'Oh dry up, you stupe!' John murmured.

'Shut up and keep still,' Jason commanded.

The passengers hung around on deck, looking uneasily at the convoy fast disappearing over the horizon. A corvette still circled round them, her signalling light winking.

'Pat can read Morse,' Andrew announced. 'What does it say, fathead?'

'What does it say, Pat?' Jean said.

'It's going back to the convoy,' Pat said. Sure enough, at that moment the corvette turned and shot away, the waves parting steeply before her. Then they were alone, a very small freighter with half a dozen gunners to protect her. Lunch time came and went. No one had much appetite. Dix did not come to table. Engineers with spanners and hammers swarmed up and down. The sound of banging replaced the reassuring beat of engines. Mrs Grant asked the boys to keep within hail, and all afternoon they remained on the deck.

'Here we are,' Andrew said, 'in the middle of the Spanish Main. There must be lots of West Indian islands about, but they're all out of sight. Suppose we had to get off in life-boats, Mrs Grant, could you draw us a chart to get to land? Did you know she was a geographer, Mr Dix?'

'Ladies can be whatever they wish to be these days,' Goldbeard answered gallantly. His tone was a trifle forced, however. He kept walking round and round the deck and staring about the horizon, until Mrs Grant wondered if he were as nervous as she was.

At tea-time, however, the sound of engines cheered them all up. There was an instant change in the feeling of the ship. Instead of pitching uncertainly on the waves, she responded to the helm once more. Mr Dix's preoccupation vanished. He ordered gingerbeer and lemonade for Mrs Grant and the boys, to celebrate their deliverance. The freighter turned and raced to overtake the convoy. Before the early tropical darkness fell they were in sight of the rear ships, and when they woke up next morning they were once more back in line.

Southwards the convoy steamed. The captain ordered a sail to be stretched between two spars, and this when filled with water made an enjoyable plunge bath on the hot afternoons. The concert, which was given on the well deck in the afternoon at Mrs Grant's suggestion, was a great success. Goldbeard was the compère. He told funny stories in between items, and made them seem twice as good. A piano had been dragged out from the dining saloon, and Mrs Grant and John played two duets which were well applauded. Andrew had offered to sing, but after an audition, Goldbeard persuaded him to hand out programmes instead. There was a comb-and-bell orchestra by the children, and one of the apprentices crooned. The Chief engineer recited from Burns; and not to be outdone, the purser gave several pieces on the musical saw. The concert ended with community singing which lasted until dark.

The next day Goldbeard organized a children's sports afternoon, ending with an obstacle race for over-forties which proved most enjoyable. Then there was the boxing contest, enlivened by Andrew's shrill shouts and cries of encouragement. Mrs Grant tried to watch it, but was glad of the opportunity to leave because Jean began to cry at the sight of people fighting. Perhaps the most exciting morning was that upon which the gun crews carried out routine firing practice with live ammunition.

At last the day came when the ships broke company: some to turn west towards the Panama Canal; some to go on to South America; and some to continue by themselves to the tiny islands for which no convoy was provided. Though the sun shone brighter than ever, and the waves were gentle and blue, the day that found them alone was a depressing one. There had been much comfort in the presence of other ships. Now their little freighter had no support. True, it was only for a couple of days that they went alone, but the seas seemed full of peril.

'It's like what they used to feel hundreds of years ago when they sailed here in the Spanish Main,' Andrew said. 'Think of Blackbeard, and Captain English, and Morgan, and Long John Silver and the other pirates!'

Mrs Grant was glad that he could excite his fancy with stories of past perils. For her, the dangers of modern warfare at sea were enough to keep her wakeful. There was no carelessness about life-jackets in those two days of their solitary progress.

'Wake up! Wake up!' Andrew called at dawn of the third day. 'We've anchored, and I can see fishing boats quite close by.'

'Are we in port already?' John asked sleepily.

'No. We have to wait for a pilot and everything,' Andrew said, tickling his feet. 'Come on, lazy louts! Shake a leg!' He hopped over the threshold of the cabin and rushed up on deck again. The others were not long in following him.

'D'you think we'll land before breakfast?' Andrew asked, as they stood watching the faint blue cloud which was Tripadoes lying on the edge of the horizon.

'Of course not,' John replied. 'They'll probably give us a special breakfast because they're sorry we're leaving.'

'Will they really?' Andrew asked, enchanted with the idea. He fished in his pockets. 'Bother!' he exclaimed, 'I must have left my notebook under my pillow.' He dashed down. The engines began to throb, and the ship turned directly towards the island. Everyone came up on deck. More sailing boats came out from the shelter of the reef, and a couple of motor boats came to circle around the ship.

Finally a pilot and some security and health officers boarded her. The sun came up, and they could see the western shore of Tripadoes, with white beaches on the north, and the palm-lined esplanade farther south. There was a vague jumble of hills inland, and as they neared the shore the harbour entrance disclosed itself, and they could see the little port within.

'I wonder where Badanda College is,' Jason said.

'Do you suppose we can see it from here?' John asked.

'Let's ask Dix to point it out.'

'I haven't seen him on deck yet,' John said.

Andrew came up.

'I can't find my notebook,' he said. 'I've looked everywhere. You haven't seen it, have you children?'

'Who are you speaking to?' Jason growled.

' "To whom are you speaking", you mean,' Andrew corrected him preparing to skip out of reach. 'I'm speaking to you two lads.'

Jason made a threatening gesture, but John said lazily,

'Run around and find Mr Dix, will you? Ask him to point out Badanda College.'

'But I can't find him. He's not in his cabin.'

'Well, he's probably on deck.'

'No he isn't. I've looked everywhere. I wanted to ask him if he'd got my notebook. I've searched all over for him.'

'He may be in the bath,' Jason said. 'Never mind. Don't bother him.'

'Jolly nice, isn't it?' Andrew said, hanging over the rail. 'It's like a picture. I suppose that's the port. Coo! It's got a narrow entrance! Do you suppose we'll get through it?'

'Stupe!' Jason exclaimed. 'Do you think they'd run for it if they thought we'd stick?'

'Good morning, everyone,' Mrs Grant said. She had come along with Jean and Guy, all dressed ready to go ashore. 'Have you boys got all your packing done?' she asked. 'If not, would you mind seeing to it as soon as breakfast is over? I'll give the smaller ones a hand if they need it. I'll come along to see if all the odds and ends are gathered up. The stewards will take our bags to the well-deck as soon as we tell them that they are packed. They say that it will be another hour before the authorities clear us and allow us to land. Hurrah! There's the breakfast gong!'

The explosion was terrific

They had flying-fish for breakfast, which tasted uncommonly good after the cold storage food of the long slow voyage in convoy. It made them all feel cheerful about their future life on the island. Afterwards Mrs Grant made them peer under their bunks and search along ledges to see that nothing was left behind. She also saw about tipping the cabin and bath and dining-room stewards. The officers and apprentices and gunners were visited, and good-byes were said. All the business of passports and health was transacted. The baggage was piled on the well deck ready to be lowered to the dock, where groups of negroes were ready to receive it. Finally the ship, which had been waiting outside the harbour entrance, received the signal to enter. Slowly it went forward. Mrs Grant and the boys stood looking eagerly at the little port which was to be the centre of their lives for an indefinite period. Even Jason relaxed his hostility towards his foster mother and became quite amiable. There was a small inner basin filled with sailing sloops and launches, and an outer wharf which was ready to deal with their ship. Beyond stretched a palm-shaded quay, and a jumble of shopping streets, some government buildings, and farther off, wooden bungalows hidden by trees.

'Well, I'm glad we've come all this way safely,' Mrs Grant said, with a great sigh of relief. 'What next, I wonder?'

The answer was so unexpected, and so quick in arriving that no one had time to turn. For at the moment when the little freighter was fairly in the harbour mouth there was a terrific impact. A torpedo fired at short range smashed into the stern, and before the vessel could settle on the sandbar completely blocking the entrance, another whizzed by and struck the wharf. Instantly all was confusion.

CHAPTER 4

Torpedoed Within Sight of Land

THE explosion was terrific. As if kicked by a gigantic foot the ship was jerked forward, and began to sink immediately in the narrowest part of the harbour entrance. As it tilted more and more to starboard, everything loose on deck went sliding down. Trunks, bags, and cases piled ready for disembarkation crashed through the handrail into the water; and after them slid everyone who could not instantly grab hold of a fixed object. A large hole had been torn in the stern immediately beneath the rear gun platform, bringing the heavy weight of armament crashing down. There the ship stuck, between the two curving arms of the breakwater, like a sluice-gate across a lock.

Mrs Grant had been standing on the starboard side with one arm around a post and the other around Guy who had been sitting on the rail. The little boy was torn from his mother's grasp, and pitched into the sea. Jean, who was not tall enough to look over the top, had woven her arms and legs through the lower rails, and when the ship tipped sideways, found herself suspended over the water. Pat and Andrew were sent rolling over and over until they crashed into the foot of the companionway leading to the officers' quarters above. Jason was thrown into the scuppers and received a nasty gash across his head. John, who had been sprawling lazily along the rail with his legs and arms spread out so that his chin could rest on the top, managed to cling on like a limpet. One of the stewards who was passing with a tray of coffee, came crashing down beside him, tray and all. There he crouched groaning, unable at first to rise.

Above the noise and confusion John heard Mrs Grant screaming, 'Guy! Guy! Guy!'

'I'll get him!' he shouted, and began to tear off his white jacket and kick off his shoes.

'Make for the stone steps just inside the harbour!' gasped the steward at his side. He pointed forward. John nodded, and dropped overboard.

The narrow space left between this side of the ship and the end of the mole was strewn with wreckage and struggling people. It was no easy task for John to reach the child, but he was a strong swimmer, and avoiding people who tried to clutch him, he grabbed Guy and started to swim into the harbour. Luckily the tide was still rising and helped him along. In a few minutes the two were out of sight of the ship inside the breakwater.

Jean was screaming with pain and fright, but in that tumult she could scarcely be heard. Her mother pulled her back and propped her against the steep slope of the deck. Andrew came crawling along the tangle of ropes and rails like an active spider over a web. By a miracle he still had his glasses on.

'Hi! Hi! Hi!' he screeched. 'The back of the ship's on fire!'

Jason, the gash on his head bleeding profusely, pulled himself towards them along the scuppers. Only Pat lay quite still under the lowest step of the companionway.

'What shall we do?' shouted Mrs Grant to the steward. 'Do you think the ship will turn over?'

The man shook his head. He had broken a rib, and the pain of breathing made him open and shut his mouth like a fish.

'We're stuck!' he gasped. 'No fear of sinking. But ship's on fire. Might be hit again. Ammunition might explode. Are you hurt?' He began painfully to loosen the life-belts from the side to drop to those struggling in the water.

'No, I'm not hurt,' answered Mrs Grant.

'Get around to the other side, then. It's nearer to the mole. They'll get a line ashore.' He groaned as he worked. 'The town's on fire!' he gasped, pointing to the shore.

The second torpedo had hit the wharf. At one moment the quay had been lined with negro dockers, officials, and friends waiting for the ship to come alongside: the next moment all who were not killed or injured were rushing in confusion away from the waterside. Smoke poured out of warehouses and customs' sheds.

The steward moved on to unfasten other lifebelts, and shouted back at Jason.

'Help the lady to the port side!'

'I'm going to stay here until I'm sure that John and Guy are safe,' Mrs Grant cried obstinately. 'Jason, get hold of Pat. I can manage Jean for a few minutes. Andrew, can you get along by yourself?'

'Yes, I can. The fire's awful! It's coming nearer!' shrieked Andrew.

'Don't wait! Don't wait!' Mrs Grant urged, waving at him to be off. Uttering shrill yaps of excitement Andrew swarmed up the slope on all fours and disappeared. 'Stop screaming, Jean, Mummie's got you!' Mrs Grant ordered, leaning as far as she could to the side in the hopes of seeing the figures of John and Guy appear on the top of the embankment.

Meanwhile, Jason crawled back to where Pat lay. Pat's eyes were open, but he made no effort to move. Passively he allowed himself to be pulled out of his corner by one leg, and then lay sprawled against Jason's knee.

'Put your arms around my neck!' Jason shouted. Pat did not reply. He lay quite limp, like a lizard when it is immobile with fear. Jason glanced desperately around. A young apprentice appeared at the window of the lounge with a rope. He could not be heard above the noise, but made signs to Mrs Grant to tie Jean to it. The little girl resisted all attempts to do this, however, screaming and clinging closer to her mother. At last Mrs Grant shouted to Jason, and gesticulated to him to use the line for Pat. Understanding her meaning, Jason fixed a loop around Pat's body, under his arms. The child passively allowed himself to be hauled up. Jason crawled behind him. He found that on the port side the hull lay exposed, the keel against the side of the mole. Already, with the assistance of the harbour men a line had been secured from the side of the ship to the iron

staunchions on top of the breakwater. In a few minutes a
rope with a swinging seat was arranged in which children
could be tied and swung ashore.

'Mrs Grant is on the other side with the little girl,' Jason
shouted into the ear of an officer.

'We'll get her. You keep charge of the little boy. Is he
hurt?'

'He won't stand up. I think he's stunned,' Jason answered.
They worked with desperate haste, for at any moment the
fire might reach the ammunition. Those who could do so
slithered down the exposed hull to the foot of the breakwater, and climbed along the ledges of coral reef upon
which it was built. Some were able to climb up the side of
the mole by means of iron rungs and the irregularities in the
stone blocks. Amongst these was Jason, who reached the
top of the mole about the same time that Pat was swung
across from the ship.

'I'll take him,' he said.

'Get him to shore as quick as you can.'

'Where shall I take him to?' Jason asked, but an impatient gesture checked him. There was no time for discus-
sion and, besides, there was only one way to shore. The
narrow stone parapet was overcrowded, and more survivors
were constantly arriving. Some were badly hurt, and had
to be carried on litters. An officer helped to place Pat on
Jason's shoulders, and he started off towards the shore.
Rough seas had shifted the blocks of which the breakwater
was made, and it was slow and rough going. Even at that
early hour in the morning the sun beat down blindingly.
Twice Jason stopped and tried to get Pat to walk; but he
slumped down like a rag doll each time. An aeroplane was
now buzzing like an angry hornet, dropping depth bombs
into the sea in hopes of settling accounts with the submarine.
Jason kept to the edge of the parapet to allow stretcher-
bearers to pass. Elderly people were being helped along by
members of the crew, and children were urged forward by
their parents. Now and then some one asked Jason if he
needed help, but he answered that he could manage. His

Half-dazed with heat he carried Pat across his shoulder

own head was still bleeding, but other people were in worse condition. He kept turning and looking back, expecting to see Mrs Grant, but there was no sign of her, nor even of Andrew, who seemed to have disappeared from the face of the earth.

When he reached the end of the mole and stepped down on to the beach, he stood aside out of the hurrying throng, feeling undecided what to do next. He did not wish to go on without the others. He felt that he should put Pat down somewhere in safety and go back to help with Jean. To his right all the buildings of the wharf were on fire. In front of him there was a stone wall with a single gate in it which was choked by a frightened mob, all trying to get away. Jason took a few steps away from the crowd, and bracing Pat against the wall, looked anxiously again down the length of the crowded breakwater, but without catching a glimpse of the others. The sun blazed down. Jason's head throbbed. He resolved to go along the narrow edge of sand in the opposite direction from the wharf, and find a shelter for Pat, and then to return and try to get back to the ship. If he went out through the gate with the crowd it was not likely that he would be allowed to return.

So, half-dazed with the heat and the pain in his head, and with the limp weight of Pat still across his shoulders he edged along the sand, which would soon be covered as the tide was rising, trying to find a way past the stone wall which ran on apparently for miles. At last the wall turned a corner, and gave place to a dense grove through which he could discover no path. He could no longer see the wharf. The sand was broader now, and smoother, and in the distance there seemed to be a village. Jason went painfully on until he came to some boats upturned on the shore; and the grove gave place to clumps of palms, and a couple of fishermen's huts. The doors were open, but no one was about, and though he shouted, no face appeared at the windows. Straggling lanes led up through thorn hedges, and along one of these Jason carried his burden. Now he heard a harsh voice singing, or rather screeching:

' "Dare to be a Daniel!
 Dare to stand alone!
 Dare to have a purpose true:
 Dare to make it known!" '

'Hello, there!' Jason shouted. A little naked black boy leading a goat came around the side of a hut. He stared at Jason, and piped out in a frightened way,

'Granmammie! Granmammie!'

The voice inside the hut had stopped short at Jason's shout.

'Can I come in?' Jason asked. He scarcely recognized his own voice, so hoarse was it from fatigue and shouting.

The child made no reply, but stared.

The voice inside the hut called,

'Joseph!'

'Yes, Granmammie,' answered the child.

'Who dat, Joseph?'

'It a white man, Granmammie.'

'What he want?'

'I dunno, Granmammie.'

'I want help,' Jason said. He pushed open the gate, and went up a sandy path lined with enormous pink sea shells and ferns, to a wooden porch, and ascended the five shaky steps which led to the verandah.

'He comin' in!' screeched the little negro. 'He comin', Granmammie.'

'Oh Lawd!' the voice said. 'Who dat? What de madder?'

Jason knocked at the door.

'Who dat?' the voice groaned. 'Who dat?'

'I want help,' Jason repeated.

'Come, come!' the voice said, between fear and curiosity.

Jason pushed open the unpainted door, and found himself standing in a small, neat room lined with bookshelves. Two rocking chairs faced the door, and against a wall stood a writing table with stacks of exercise books on it.

'Who you is?' the voice demanded, and Jason realized that it came from an inner room, separated by a partition in which was an arch veiled with a curtain made of strings

of beads which swayed slightly in the breeze with a contin-
uous clashing rattle. Evidently he could be seen through
this bead curtain, and the sight must have been reassuring,
for the voice continued in a more confident tone, 'You
want de mister? But he gone to see what is de noise. But
come, come.'

After a moment's hesitation Jason crossed the room
which shook under his tread as if on uncertain beams, and
parted the bead curtains. A pair of eyes stared at him out of
a face so black that he could scarcely distinguish it from the
gloom of a great bed. The windows of the room were
shuttered, and closely draped with pink lace curtains. After
the glare of the sunlight outside Jason felt as blind as a bat.

'Come, come,' the voice repeated. 'You ain' frighten, eh?
I only a old woman. I in bed. What de matter wit de little
boy?'

'We've come off a ship,' Jason said. 'It's been hit by a
submarine in the harbour, and I have brought the boy
ashore.'

'Oh laws!' the old woman groaned. 'Dat de noise, eh?
Boom! Boom! crash! De chile hurt?'

'I don't think so,' Jason answered.

'Put he down,' the old woman said in a gentler tone.
'Poor ting! So small, and frighten, eh? Dere a chair. Oh laws!
You haid bleedin'.'

'It's nothing,' Jason said, his voice sliding faintly up into
a treble whisper. He lowered Pat on to the chair, and
touched his own head which was sticky with blood.

'Joseph! Where dat chile?' the old negress exclaimed.
'Joseph!'

'I here, Granmammie!' piped the little boy.

'You take de white mister and let he wash he haid,' the old
woman ordered. 'He show you where de pipe,' she added.
Jason turned and stumbled after the black child. He felt
suddenly sick, and hoped that he could control himself until
he could get out of the hut. He had barely time to reach the
garden before he was sick. The child watched him, and when
he had straightened up again, he pointed to a tap by the

side of the gate. Jason turned the water on and let it run over his head and hands until he felt better. Joseph, who had been recalled into the hut by his grandmother now reappeared with a clean towel. Jason dried his hands, and winding the towel around his head to try to staunch the flow of blood, he went up into the house again.

'I must go back to find the others,' he said, 'Can I leave this boy here?'

'Of course, of course!' the old woman said. 'He all right. Leave he.'

'You'll stay here, Pat, until we come to get you?' Jason asked.

Pat did not answer. He still sat where Jason had put him, but in the latter's absence he had put one arm upon a small table, and was touching the knob of a portable radio set that stood on it.

'De radio don' work,' the old woman chuckled. 'For long it work, but now since a week it don' say nuttin. It mus' fix.'

Pat still sat silent, but he stroked the knob, and turned it slightly.

'Well, good-bye, then,' Jason said. 'Thank you,' he added to the old woman. 'I'll be back as soon as I can.'

'Well,' she said, 'he all right wit we. Don' to worry.'

Jason still hesitated, staring at Pat. But the boy did not look at him. He seemed quite indifferent to being left, and with a sort of perplexed anger Jason left him.

Once more out in the lane Jason's headache returned with renewed violence. The sun scorched down. He started off in the direction which he thought he remembered having come from, but in a few paces was brought up short by a fallen palm. This certainly had not blocked his path before. He went back, tried again, and in a few moments was quite lost. This time he could not even find his way back to the hut. He was almost blind with pain and sun-glare when he reached a clearing in the tangle of trees and hedges, and found himself on the edge of a common which sloped up in a series of ledges to a ridge where he could see houses sticking up between trees. A road led down the slope, and along it was creaking a cart drawn by a donkey. A young negro sat dangling his legs from the shafts. He kept casting uneasy glances back over his shoulder, and when Jason stepped into the road he pulled up with an exclamation of fear.

'Will you give me a lift in your cart?' Jason asked as firmly as he could.

'Where you wants to go?' the young negro countered.

'To the harbour.'

'No, I ain' goin' dere. De police turn all de traffic away from de town. A German fleet shellin' de harbour, man.'

'But I must get back,' said Jason faintly.

'No goin' back,' the man declared. 'You want I should be kill, eh?'

'Where are you going now?' Jason asked. The world was swirling around him, but he heard the answer,

'I goin' to de College.'

'Take me there,' Jason stammered. He flung himself, or fell, into the low cart, and lost consciousness.

CHAPTER 5

Confusion and Doubt

THE small children were being swung ashore one by one
in a sort of canvas swing. Andrew was quick to see that if
his elders once laid hands on him he would lose the fearful
joy of sliding down the hull of the ship. He might never
have such a chance again! Without hesitation he slipped
through the rails, and, half-sliding, half-rowing himself
with his hands, he reached the keel before he could be
ordered not to make the attempt. The coral ledges upon
which the breakwater was built were crowded now with
those who had escaped, and who were taking their turn to
clamber up the iron rungs to the embankment. Not being
tall, Andrew could not pull himself up the irregular blocks
of masonry as Jason had done. Impatient of waiting his
turn, and fearful that they might even yet haul him up like
a parcel, he headed seawards along the reef to look for an
easier way up. In a few minutes he had turned the corner
and was out of sight of the ship. The ledges outside the
harbour were much more battered by the seas, and he
climbed for some distance before he found that he was no
nearer to the top of the mole. An overhang of rock made it
impossible for him to work his way further upwards. Even
in that calm sea the rhythmic beat of the swell splashed
spray on his glasses and if the wind should drive the waves
in harder, he would certainly be washed from the ledge or
crack along which he was crawling. He looked out, but
could see nothing but blue sea, until presently an aeroplane
came zooming overhead, and swooped lower in widening
circles.

'Depth bombs!' Andrew shouted. 'Oh, gosh!' Until then he
had heard no sounds except the drag and splash of the waves;
but just as he was deciding that he had better go back and
climb up the ladder with all the rest of the survivors, he

heard the stuttering of an outboard motor, and looking cautiously down, saw a small boat coming into sight. In it sat Goldbeard, dressed immaculately in white, with a sun helmet. He was staring ahead with a strained, astonished look.

'Hi!' Andrew shouted. 'Hi! Mr Dix!' He threw a stone which bounced on the side of the boat and then hit Goldbeard hard on the nose. Goldbeard said something violent and looked up. He saw Andrew clinging to the ledge. Though his eyes were still watering with the force of the blow, he slowed down the engine, and drove the little boat as close to the sea wall as he could. Then, still grasping the tiller with his right hand, he threw Andrew a line with his left. Andrew seized it.

'Climb down,' Dix shouted. 'It's slippery, so come carefully.' The lower, broken ledges were green with seaweed and swarming with crabs.

'Out of my way!' Andrew shouted at them. If he slipped down amongst them, what a nipping he would get from all those claws!

'They won't hurt you! Come on!' Dix shouted. He had grasped a point of rock, and was steadying the boat while he pulled the slackening rope in. 'The water's not deep on that ledge. Come on!'

Andrew waded nervously through a couple of yards of sea, and stepped into the boat.

'What happened to the ship? ... Where are the others, I mean?' Goldbeard asked.

'Mrs Grant was still on board when I left,' Andrew said. 'Guy fell overboard, and John jumped after him. He's swimming to the other side of the harbour. Mrs Grant told me to go on by myself because of the fire. I wasn't swung ashore, Mr Dix, I went by myself ...'

As if he did not wish to listen, Goldbeard opened the throttle and the engine roared as the little boat dashed to the harbour entrance. The wind was carrying smoke and flames forward over the little ship. There was a narrow passage on the starboard side, where there was room for a small boat to get past. Heedless of the danger of explosion, he headed close under the overhanging side. So short a time had elapsed since Andrew's departure that survivors were still streaming ashore from the port side.

'There's Mrs Grant and Jean,' Andrew shrieked. There they were in the same place, braced against the tilting deck with their feet in the scuppers, and Jean was still wailing. A couple of officers were putting a belt around her. Goldbeard drove his craft close under the rail.

'Let them down into my boat!' he shouted. The officers agreed instantly. Every moment was precious. The ship might blow up. There might be other attempts to torpedo her. Though Jean clung to her mother and never stopped crying for a moment, it was not long before they were both lowered into the boat.

'But where are the others?' Dix asked, his hand still on the side of the steamer.

'They've gone!' Mrs Grant answered. She pointed into the harbour. Dix immediately started up again, and Mrs Grant directed him to skirt the other arm of the breakwater. They did so until they reached the first flight of stone steps, where they saw John sitting with Guy beside him. Both looked exhausted. The little boy began to cry when he saw his mother, and stretched out his arms.

'But where are the others?' Dix asked in a tone more agitated than ever. 'Where's Pat?'

'Jason took him,' Mrs Grant said. 'He must have got him ashore from the other side.'

Dix muttered an exclamation, and looked across the harbour. They could see passengers and crew streaming along the opposite arm of the breakwater towards the shore. While he gazed at them as if searching for the two missing boys, John came down the steps with Guy, and Mrs Grant took her child into her arms.

'Good old Jonathan!' Andrew shouted, giving John a cheeky pat on the back.

Jean looked resentfully at her brother, and gave him a push.

'He's all wet,' she sobbed. 'Don't let him sit on your lap, Mummie! He's all wet!'

'Shall we all get out and walk to shore?' Mrs Grant asked. Dix shook himself out of his unpleasant tangle of thoughts.

'No, no,' he answered. 'I'll take you all along to the wharf. The buildings are on fire, but you can see that the police are directing people towards the left gate. Get in, John.' He gave another tortured glance back.

'How ever did you get hold of this boat?' Mrs Grant asked. Dix did not answer.

'I wondered that, too!' Andrew piped out. 'How did you get off so soon to be able to get it, Mr Gold ... Mr Dix ... You must have been the very first off, weren't you?'

Dix made no reply. His whole attention seemed to be concentrated on driving the boat across the harbour at top speed. The pier was in confusion. Dix made the boat fast to an iron ring at the foot of the steps.

'They're making everyone go through that gate,' Dix said. 'The one I pointed out before. Keep an eye skinned for the others, Andrew. I'll carry Guy. All right.'

'But I'm wet already, and so is he,' John protested. 'You'll get your suit all wet ...'

'Never mind, I say!' Dix said impatiently. His immaculate white suit did not look as if it had come from a torpedoed ship. He held out his arms for the little boy, and led the way up. John helped Mrs. Grant out, and took Jean's hand. Andrew, of course, reached the top of the steps first.

'I can't see them anywhere,' he said. 'Shall I run back to see if they are still there waiting for us?'

'No you don't,' Dix shouted. 'Catch hold of him, John.'

'Let go!' Andrew said. 'I'm not a baby.'

'You are,' John said in a tired, but still good-natured voice.

'*Please*, Andrew, keep with us!' Mrs Grant begged.

'Come along there! Hurry!' a harbour policeman shouted, waving at them.

There was no choice now. Soldiers and volunteers had formed a cordon along the wharf, and were directing everyone to the gate. Mr Dix asked if Jason and Pat had gone through, and was assured that they must have done so. The fire was spreading rapidly from the wharves to the town, and there seemed little hope of stopping it, for the shops were made of wood and the streets were so narrow that the flames leapt them, fanned by the brisk sea breeze. The roadways were filled with people trying to save their belongings. There was no lingering here. The resources of the island were pressed into service. The two fire engines, the police, volunteers with hand pumps and buckets, and members of the Red Cross and Ambulance services: all did their best. The survivors, pushed along in kindly haste, were given temporary shelter in a school building well outside the town. Those who had been hurt were taken on stretchers to the hospital, or given first aid; children were sorted out, and comforted; and those whose clothing had suffered were given what could be found to fit them from the stores which had been collected for an emergency of this kind. But nowhere amongst the crowd could Pat and Jason be seen.

Foremost amongst the helpers was Lady May Smith, the Governor's wife, a short, jovial woman whose white curls bristled with energy. She walked at the head of a small band of helpers, giving orders which were eagerly carried out. At the beginning of the war she had prepared for just such a disaster, and now all her committees were moving like parts of well-oiled machinery. In due course Lady May spoke to Mrs Grant, and asked her if she had all that she needed to make her comfortable. Mrs Grant thanked her and assured her that she had; but told her of her anxiety about Jason and Pat. Mr Dix, unaccountably silent, stood in the background with Guy, who had been put into dry clothing, asleep in his arms.

'If they were seen to get off the ship, they'll be all right,' Lady May said emphatically. 'They couldn't possibly come to any harm on the island. They've taken shelter somewhere.

C

How old is the bigger boy? Fourteen? Well, he's old enough to take care of the little one. I'll send out the scouts to look for him. That's a thing they will love.' She turned to the nearest devoted follower, a pale, earnest girl in spectacles, and said, 'Just make a note for me, will you, of the two boys who are missing.'

At this point Andrew, who had been talking to everyone, dashed up with a young parson in tow.

'Here's Mr Jones from Badanda College,' he piped. 'He came to meet us, and they told him to come here.'

'Harry Jones, just the *very* person we wanted,' Lady May beamed. 'Now, Mrs ... er ...' she looked at her notes, '... Grant. You'll be all right. Harry will take care of you. Have you your car, Harry? Can they go with you at once?'

Mr Jones blushed. He could never quite get used to Lady May's informal habit of calling people by their first names, and it always flustered him.

'Er ... As a matter of fact,' he stammered, 'I er ... that is, I had it beside the wharf; but what happened to it I can't tell. The police won't let me go back to see.'

'What's the number? I'll go back and see if it's O.K.,' Andrew offered.

'You're a really helpful boy!' Lady May cooed. 'But not this time,' she shook a waggish finger at him. 'And who do you belong to, young man?'

'I'm Andrew Thomson, and I am with Mrs Grant.'

'Ah yes, I have you down!' Lady May said putting her pencil with great heartiness through a name on her list. 'Mrs Grant, Jean Grant, Guy Grant ... Which one is he?'

'There he is. Mr Dix has got him,' Andrew said.

'Where? Why Charley Dix, when did you come back? On this boat? You look like a survivor right enough.' Guy's wet clothes had spoiled Goldbeard's immaculate appearance. He did not appear to be in his usual jovial spirits, but he made an effort to seem concerned only to get Guy and his mother into more comfortable surroundings.

'Yes, I am here, May,' he said, making shy Mr Jones envious by his easy familiarity with the leader of Island society. 'I'm going on to my house as soon as I see that Mrs Grant and her little lot are settled.'

'But do you have to carry that great boy? Let me have him. We'll find a small chair and he can sit by his mother.'

'I'll just hang on to him,' Goldbeard said as Guy, awakened in the midst of this confusion, lifted up his voice and roared at the idea of being taken by a stranger.

'Give him a lollipop, Margy,' Lady May said, waving to another girl with a basket of sweets who was going the rounds of the children. 'Now, let's see ... which are the ones that are missing ...'

'Jason and Pat,' piped up Andrew who had bobbed up under Lady May's arm to have a look at her list.

'Ah, yes!' Lady May put a question mark beside both names. 'Then there is John. Where is he?'

'There he is!' Andrew cried, darting behind Mr Dix and dragging John out. 'He saved Guy's life this morning!'

'Did he indeed?' Lady May exclaimed. 'Well, you'll have to tell me all about it another time ...'

'And he's a musical genius,' Andrew concluded.

'Well, well! Fine!' Lady May exclaimed giving the list back to her secretary, a graceful, long-nosed lady who followed so close behind that she almost breathed down her neck. 'So you are a musician, John? What do you play?'

'The piano,' John said, unclasping his hand from Andrew's and going quietly back to his obscure position again.

'Do make a note of that,' Lady May said to her secretary. 'We're always needing people to play for us. As for you, Andrew, I think we'll have to make you into a special messenger.'

'Can I start now?' Andrew asked eagerly. 'I'm not a bit tired. I can find my way to Badanda College later on by myself. I'm good at finding my way.'

'You'll have to wait until I find you a commission and a

special bag. King's Messengers always have special bags, you know. You'll have to have one of a particular sort.'

'Oh, thank you!' Andrew exclaimed.

'And now that you have your group, you'll want to get away, Harry,' Lady May said. 'If it's only a car you need, there are a few volunteers waiting to drive.'

'I'll go along with them,' Dix said. Mrs Grant got up and prepared to follow with Jean and John. Andrew had a last word.

'If you forget about the commission I'll remind you!' he said to Lady May.

'Splendid! Splendid!' Lady May beamed. 'Mrs Grant, I hope that you will be able to get a good rest. Don't worry. I'll send you some clothes. Let me know how you all get on.' She waved a gracious hand, and moved on to others.

'Andrew is blissfully happy,' Mrs Grant remarked to Goldbeard as she followed Mr Jones and Andrew out of the schoolroom. 'He loves to be an attendant sprite.'

'He'll get all he likes in that line,' Dix answered. Mrs Grant was so tired that she was near tears, but she could see that he was not his usual self.

'Do you think that Lady May is right about the boys?' she asked. 'Can there be anything to worry about? I'm in charge of them, and I do feel that they are my own special responsibility. But I don't know the island at all. How could she say that no harm could come to them? What I am afraid of is that they might have been trapped in one of the burning buildings, not that they might get into danger outside the town.'

'I understand what you mean,' Dix said. 'But you must try not to worry. Here's the car.'

'If you are going up to the College with Mrs Grant there won't really be room for me,' Mr Jones said. 'I think I'll go back to Lady May and see if I can be of any further service.'

It was arranged that Goldbeard should drive, with John beside him. Guy, Mrs Grant, Jean and Andrew would be able to squeeze in behind. Andrew, in fact, did not sit down at all, but stood leaning over the driver ready to see and ask questions about everything.

'Have we got far to go?' he demanded.

'No, not far.'

'How far?'

'About seven miles.'

'I think that's a long way.'

'It is when you walk: but it won't take us long by car.'

'Which direction do we go?'

'Almost due north.'

'Is the College on the beach?'

'On a ridge overlooking the sea.'

'Is that it over there?'

'No. That's a hotel. There it is, farther on, with a red roof.'

'Golly! It looks fine. Look, John, there's the school. Look, John!'

'I heard you. I see it,' John said quietly.

'Look, Jean, there's the school.'

'I don't want to look,' muttered Jean who was determined to be cross. 'Mummie, I want a drink. I want a drink *now*.'

'Hush, Jean,' Mrs Grant said. 'You'll get a drink directly. We'll soon be at the school.'

'I don't want to go to school! I want to go home!' Jean sobbed.

The car slowed, and turned off the main road at right angles.

'Oh, look, there's the sea. Golly! We're going to drive straight off the cliff!' Andrew exclaimed.

Fortunately he was wrong. The road led down steeply for a few yards over the crest of the hill, and then turned to the right. A gravel drive led between hibiscus hedges into a large garden. Beyond it they could see the white, arcaded buildings of the College.

'There's a cart in the way,' Andrew said.

An old, donkey-drawn cart was proceeding at a slow pace in front of them. The driver looked back over his shoulder and shook his head to show that there was no chance of passing, and that he could go no faster.

'There's someone lying down in the cart,' Andrew said, standing up in the open car and looking ahead. 'It's a man ... it's a boy ... It's Jason!'

Dix stopped the car so suddenly that his passengers were pitched forward somewhat roughly. Andrew, who by this time was hanging over the side, went out on his head. He regained his feet in a moment, picked up his glasses and ran forward; but Goldbeard got there first.

'*There's someone lying down in the cart,*' said Andrew

'He's dead! He's sick! Look at his head, it's bleeding!' Andrew cried.

Dix was shaking Jason by the shoulder. 'He's fainted,' he said to Mrs Grant who had hurried up.

'Where's the other one ... the little boy,' he asked the negro driver.

'Only he, Boss,' the negro said. 'I ain' see no other.'

'Where did he come from?'

'Down yander,' the driver said, pointing down towards the beach with his whip. 'He come from de roadside, and say he want I to take he to de harbour. I tell he dat de police won' let anyone go dere. De whole town on fire. He ask me where I goin? I say, de College. He say, "Take me dere" and fall in. So I come, and I never see no one else.'

'They've got him, then,' Dix groaned as if to himself, 'They've got him, then, the devils!'

CHAPTER 6

The Mystery Deepens

AFTER his extraordinary exclamation, Dix said no more. Jean and Guy began to cry. Even Andrew felt his tongue freeze with not unpleasant terror: but not for long.

'What devils, Goldbe ... Mr Dix?' he asked. 'Do you believe that there are real ones? I mean here? Are there special ones on tropical islands, and are they after Pat?'

Mrs Grant tried to explain to the driver of the cart.

'There was another little boy,' she said slowly and distinctly. 'A little boy like this one.' She pointed to Andrew who was speechless with indignation for a moment.

'I'm *much* bigger than Pat!' he protested. 'He's only up to my eyebrow.'

'I ain't see only he,' the negro repeated again and again.

'Well, let's go on to the College,' Mrs Grant suggested, looking with some surprise at Mr Dix, who seemed sunk in painful thought. 'Jason must be put to bed at once.' She put her hand on the head of the unconscious boy in the cart. 'He's got a high temperature,' she said to Dix.

Goldbeard roused himself.

'Of course we must get him into bed,' he said. 'Jacob, drive up to the porch. I'll come behind.'

'We might as well walk, since we're out, and it's only a few steps,' Mrs Grant said, taking the reluctant Jean by the hand. Guy screamed to be allowed to go back into the car, so they put him in with John, who had not left his seat. He was perhaps more concerned than any of them with Jason's condition, but it was not like him to fuss. 'There's nothing I can do,' he thought, 'so I might as well keep out of the way.'

'I'll go ahead and ring the bell,' Andrew shouted, sprinting ahead of the cart as it started up once more. There was no need to ring, however. The sound of wheels had brought a score of little boys on to the verandahs. As he reached the steps a pleasant-faced lady with white hair, dressed in a white uniform, came out of the door. Andrew's hand shot out and grasped hers.

'Here we are!' he said breathlessly. 'Our ship was torpedoed in the harbour, but we got off all right; but Pat's lost and Jason's hurt. He's in the cart.'

To this scrambled account Miss Hall, the matron, for she was the lady in uniform, gave a bewildered hearing.

'Mrs Grant's walking along, and Goldbeard's driving,' Andrew went on.

'Who?'

'Mr Dix. We always call him Goldbeard, don't you?'

'I haven't yet,' said Miss Hall with a chuckle.

'And the little girl that's crying is Jean. She generally cries,' said Andrew with a superior air. To his disgust Miss Hall hurried forward and as there was only room for one to squeeze past as the donkey cart went by, she was the first to greet the newcomers. However, Andrew discovered that all the little boys had followed behind, and he was more than pleased to answer their eager questions.

'We heard the noise,' they said. 'Oh ho! What a noise!' 'Were you on board, man?' 'How did you get off?' 'Are you coming to live at the school?' Andrew was in his element. Miss Hall shouted for the boys to summon the servants; but there was no need. Hearing the excitement, they came running from the back of the house, eager to know what was going on.

In this eddy of boys and servants the cart drew up at the foot of the steps, and the car stopped behind it. Mrs Grant had a few hurried words with Miss Hall, who was all astonishment and sympathy.

'We heard the crash,' she said, 'while we were having prayers. All the masters have gone, for there was a call at once for the volunteers. Did you see Mr Jones? He went to get you. But let's not talk until we get this poor boy to bed. We'll take him up to the infirmary at once. Millie!' she called to the oldest maid, 'call the doctor.'

'The telephone don' work, Madam.'

'Then two of you scouts ... you, Victor, and you, Robin, get on your bicycles and ride to the doctor's house.'

'He's sure to be at the harbour, Miss Hall. They've called up all the doctors, they say. Shall we go to town?'

'No, no! The police won't let you through. Go to the house, and leave word for him to come as soon as he returns.'

'John, if you'll take Jason's feet I can manage his head,' said Dix. 'Gently on to the stretcher, now.' Some of the larger boys were proud to help carry the stretcher up to the infirmary, treading with extreme softness, and talking in whispers.

All this time Jason lay without movement. He was breathing heavily; but when they rolled him on to the stretcher and carried him up to the cubicle in the top verandah which was kept as a sick room, he gave no sign of knowing that he was being moved. Miss Hall gently attended to the deep gash on his head, and saw that he was made comfortable. Millie, the old coloured nannie, was then left in charge of him in case he regained consciousness before the doctor arrived.

'Now, Mrs Grant,' Miss Hall said. 'At last I can see to you. Poor children! They must be tired. And so must you. Well, your quarters are quite ready for you. Come along.'

'Don't we live here in the school-house?' Mrs Grant asked in surprise, as her hostess started to lead her down the verandah steps.

'The boys do, of course; but I thought you'd like it better by yourselves. We've put you in that little bungalow down the steps.' She pointed out a small wooden house just below the crest of the steep hill, and then proceeded to lead the way down the narrow path towards it.

'How lovely!' Mrs Grant sighed.

'It's very small.'

The bungalow was built amongst the trees, with a marvellous view of the sea which, because of the steepness of the slope, seemed almost beneath them. There was a verandah, a tiny screened dining-room, and two bedrooms.

'I think it's ideal!' Mrs Grant said contentedly. 'If only I had my trunks, and knew where Pat was, I'd be perfectly happy.'

'Pat is sure to be found soon,' Miss Hall told her comfortingly. 'You will have your early breakfast here, and the rest of your meals in the dining hall, if that suits you. Lady May will doubtless send some clothes for you. In the meantime I will send you some of mine, and a couple of pairs of pyjamas for the children from the school stock.'

'I'll put the children to sleep, and come up to the house,' Mrs Grant said. 'Perhaps when John has settled in he would come down here and stay with them to give me a chance to come up.'

Miss Hall went away promising to send John. Jean and Guy were very cross and tired. They clung to their mother with every step she took, as though after such fearful experiences they could not bear to let her out of their sight. The water in the shower was quite warm, and after they had had a good bath they were persuaded to lie down, and were soon asleep. When John found his way down to the bungalow, Mrs Grant was waiting for him.

'The children are both asleep,' she said in a low tone. 'I wonder if you'd mind sitting here on the verandah in case they wake up? I must go to see about Jason. And is there any news of Pat?'

'No,' John said. 'And Jason is much the same.'

When Mrs Grant had departed John lowered himself into the hammock on the verandah with a great sense of relief. He was tired; and his anxiety about Pat felt worse because he could not talk it over with Jason. What had happened to him? John was going to feel out of it at Badanda, where the boys were, for the most part, much younger than himself. Andrew was in his element, of course. It was lucky John and Jason had taken to each other at once; now they would be thrown together still more because of their age. But if Jason was going to be really ill it would be a lonely time for John.

After the incessant beat of the engines in the weeks at sea, it seemed very still and quiet here. It was fine being in the open after the long voyage cramped in the tiny cabin of the freighter. John put his arms beneath his head and swung gently to and fro. The voices of boys at play were subdued by distance. This little bungalow amongst the trees was like an eagle's nest, it was so high.

'"The wrinkled sea beneath him crawls,
    He watches from his castle walls..."'
John said to himself. Though the air was warm a cool breeze caressed his cheek. The murmur of the sea and the rustle of the trees soothed him, and he fell into a peaceful doze.

Mrs Grant found the doctor, Dr Thorne, and the Head-master, the Rev Mr Boomhill, talking in low tones to Mr Dix just outside the infirmary, and in a few minutes Miss Hall and Mr Jones joined them. There was no change in Jason's condition, and no news of Pat.

'I do not think that we should be unduly worried about the missing child,' Mr Boomhill said in the smooth, reason-ing tone which he had got into the habit of using when talking to the boys. 'After all, a good many passengers saw er ... Jason carrying him along the breakwater. They must have reached the shore safely. There was no other way to go.'

'Then how is it that we've heard nothing of him?' Dix broke in. 'And why is this boy in his present condition? Pat may have fallen into the hands of ... of ... anyone. By this time he might be miles away ...'

Mr Boomhill raised his eyebrows and the whole top of his white scalp moved forward disapprovingly. 'Really, Dix,' he said, 'you are talking in a most melodramatic manner. This is not a savage island. Do you imagine that anyone here would take the trouble to kidnap him?'

'It's more likely that when everyone was rushing through the town, he might have been knocked down and badly hurt,' suggested Mr Jones. 'That's what I am worried about.'

'That's exactly what I meant,' Dix said in a low, tense voice. 'We don't know how far Jason carried him ...'

'They may never have gone through the gate at all,' said the doctor. 'It was fully half an hour before the authorities got things into order and made a cordon along the wharf. No one seems to have seen them after they arrived there and a good many people are still missing.'

'As for Jason's head,' Mrs Grant put in, 'he was hurt before he left the ship. I remember seeing his head bleeding as he crawled along the deck. He was pitched head-first into the scuppers. I saw him.'

'But surely,' Dix addressed himself to the doctor, 'you can do something ... Can't you try to revive Jason? I tell you every moment may count. Give him something! If he could only answer one question, as to where he last saw Pat, or who took him ... If you'd let me ...'

'I cannot allow anything of the kind,' Dr Thorne said. 'I'm rather surprised at you, Dix. Don't you realize that the lad is very ill? His temperature is very high. Even if you could wake him, he would not be able to give you a rational answer. You must wait.'

'Well, let me stay in his room and ask him when he is conscious ...'

'Certainly not. I have given my orders,' Dr Thorne repeated.

'And in the meantime,' Mr Dix protested violently, 'we don't know where this child Pat is, and he may be in the greatest danger. It is terribly important. I tell you we can't afford to lose time.'

Both Dr Thorne and Mr Boomhill began to look at Goldbeard with some perplexity. The doctor was a lean, kind-looking man with brown hair and a small brown moustache. He was very sunburnt, and his white suit made him look even browner. Mr Boomhill, in a grey alpaca suit with clerical collar, was as tall as Dr Thorne, but much heavier. He had thick white hair, blue eyes, and a rather obstinate face. His eyebrows and moustache were white and bristly. Harry Jones was small, and wore glasses. His chin ran away from his face into his rather long neck which seemed longer because he, too, wore a clerical collar. He was clean-shaven, with a small snub nose. But what he lacked in nose and chin he made up in Adam's apple which slid up and down nervously as he talked. Mr Jones hated to take sides, and now he looked from side to side as though trying to agree with both parties at once.

'You know the island better than any of us,' Mr Boomhill said in a voice stiff with annoyance although he tried to make it sound patient. 'You know very well that there could not possibly be anyone here who would wish to hurt the child. It will soon be dark, but someone is sure to find him. He cannot be far away: he must be somewhere between the College and the port. He is not a baby who might fall into the sea or anything like that. How old is he exactly?' he asked Mrs Grant.

'Eight,' she replied.

'Quite old enough to know his name and where he was going. He'll soon be found, and brought in by someone. Be reasonable. The people in the little villages along the shore are peaceful, ordinary workers. They bring their fish and vegetables and eggs up to us regularly.'

'All our servants live in this area,' Miss Hall put in. 'We'll tell them to keep their ears open. You know what gossips they are. If Pat is wandering around anywhere we'll soon get news of him.'

'Of course we'll send out search parties,' added Mr Boomhill. 'I can't stay myself, as I am needed to help fight the fire in the town. But I will send the older boys out with the gardener, with torches, to search the woods along the shore.'

'I must be getting back to the town, too,' said Dr Thorne. 'There are scores of people hurt, and not a few killed.'

'We need all the help possible,' Mr Boomhill agreed. 'Instead of worrying about this child, Dix, you'd better come back with us.'

'I am afraid I have urgent private affairs,' Dix replied, and his red-gold beard seemed like a shield behind which he was concealing something. He did not look at Mr Boomhill.

'So have we all,' the Headmaster returned, displeased.

Dix made no reply. Instead, he turned on his heel and went down to the car which his chauffeur had brought to take him back to his own house. It was now dusk, and as he drove away the lights of his car could be seen turning and twisting through the trees.

'Well,' said Mr Boomhill, 'I confess I am at a loss to understand our friend's attitude.'

'I am very grateful to him for taking us in his boat this morning,' Mrs Grant said, thinking that she should stick up for Dix.

'What do you mean?' Mr Boomhill asked. 'Was he not on the ship with you when the accident occurred?'

'I suppose he must have been. Where else could he have been? But yet he came along in his own boat and took us off.'

'I expect he had it sent up to the harbour to meet him,' Mr Jones suggested in his rather high voice.

'As I said before,' said Mr Boomhill, 'I really am quite at a loss . . . Well, I can't stay any longer. Miss Hall, can you provide Mrs Grant with what she needs for to-night? I leave you in charge. Get the boys to go to their dormitories quietly. Jason must not be disturbed. Very unfortunate! I knew his father years ago. Remind everyone to get up quietly to-morrow, too. I hope to be back before late breakfast, but I am prepared to spend the night down there if the fire is not soon under control. I promised Lady May that I would take charge of the emergency quarters. I think we'd better give the boys a holiday to-morrow. The masters won't be back, or if they are, they'll be very tired. Let the boys go to the beach soon after early breakfast, Miss Hall – but I leave everything to you. Good-bye for now, Mrs Grant. I trust that you will not be too tired or worried to sleep. You must take it easy to-morrow. And about Pat, don't fret. He's sure to turn up all right. I fully expect him to be here before I am in the morning. Ask for anything that you need.'

'I'll see that she gets what she needs,' Miss Hall interrupted with good nature. She seemed the only person who was not in awe of the Headmaster.

'Well, good-night ladies,' said Mr Boomhill, and actually went at last with Mr Jones.

'Can I be of service in nursing Jason to-night?' Mrs Grant asked. 'John could sleep down at the bungalow with my two.'

'No, thank you,' Miss Hall answered. 'Millie, the old nurse, is very trustworthy. She's been here longer than I have, and would be most annoyed if she were not allowed to take full charge of him at night. That is one of her duties. You have been through so much during the past twelve hours that you will need a good night's rest. Jason will have the best of care.'

'Now that Mr Boomhill is gone I don't mind confessing that I am worrying less about Jason than about Pat,' Mrs Grant said. 'I quite understand Mr Dix's anxiety, I think. You see, he is such a strange child. If Andrew were missing I wouldn't worry for a moment. He would be certain to turn up trumps. But Pat is queer.'

'Do you mean ... not normal in any way?'

'Certainly not. He is extraordinarily bright. Too bright, in some ways; but in practical things he is more helpless than Guy.'

'Well,' Miss Hall said, 'I hope he is not the type of child who is unhappy in a boarding school.'

'I don't mean that, either,' Mrs Grant said. 'I can't describe him to you, because I can't remember having seen such a child before.'

'Anyhow, try not to worry about him,' Miss Hall said. 'If you will go back to your bungalow I'll send your dinner down to you on a tray. Will the children want anything more to-night? No? Are you sure? You have an electric refrigerator, you know, and there is some milk and butter in it, and some biscuits and a few things in your cupboard in case you need them. Don't come up here again. The boys will be all right.'

'Thank you very much,' Mrs Grant said gratefully. 'I'll send John up. Good-night.'

Mrs Grant walked down the steps in the dusk feeling very

tired. She found John fast asleep in the hammock on the verandah of her bungalow, and she had some difficulty in rousing him. He was still dizzy with sleep as he walked up to the main building. No black-out had been imposed on the island, and the light streamed out of the french windows of the verandahs. The white building in its gardens seemed like an enchanted place. Moonflowers were unfurling their green-white petals to the rising moon. John lingered to look at them, and to enjoy their fragrance. But he was not left in peace for more than a minute.

'Here you are at last, you old slow-coach!' Andrew shrieked, sticking his head over the top verandah. 'Come up and tell the fellows about the time our steering gear went wrong and we almost lost the convoy . . .'

'Get away,' John said in a low tone. 'Why can't you shut up? I'm tired.'

Luckily the supper bell rang at that moment, and John saw to it that Andrew did not have a chance to resume his entreaties that evening.

CHAPTER 7

Exploring the Island

ANDREW was the first to wake up next morning. He was roused by a beam of sunlight shining through the shutters on to his eyes. Sitting up in bed beneath his mosquito net he felt under the pillow for his glasses, and when he had put them on, he stared around at the large, airy room full of sleeping boys. After the cabin, the dormitory seemed immense, and very quiet and firm. After so many weeks at sea it was strange to be on land. It seemed odd to be in a bed that did not shift from side to side or from end to end.

Andrew was too active to remain still for long, but as a newcomer he did not care to risk waking anyone up. Cautiously he pulled his net loose, and tiptoed across to the locker where his clothes were. It was the work of a moment to slip out of his night things into his shirt and shorts. Then, with his sandals in his hand, he went soundlessly down the stairs. Not a soul stirred in the building, but in the servants' quarters at the back he could hear low voices. He let himself out at a french window and went to see who was up.

'Good marnin'! You early, man,' Old Dinah the cook said. She was a stout, smiling negress with her head tied up in a red kerchief. 'What yous name?' she asked.

'Andrew Thompson.'

'Andrew, eh? And what make you get up so early, Andrew?'

'The sun woke me,' Andrew explained. 'Is it always as hot as this?'

'Hot? Oho, it not hot now. It cool,' the black woman chuckled. 'You take care not to catch col'.'

Andrew's eyes lingered on the long tables on the back verandah where trays of melons and oranges and bananas were arranged.

'Are those for breakfast?' he asked politely.

'Oho! Hungry, man?' Old Dinah said. 'Here!' She pulled some bananas from a great hand that swung from the end of the verandah, and held out a basket of oranges. 'Wait, I give you a hot drink to keep you from catchin' col',' she continued, pouring him out a bowl of steaming cocoa. 'Here a bit of bread,' she added, giving him a buttered roll.

'Thank you very much,' Andrew said, sitting down happily on the step and eating with sharp appetite. 'This is fine.' He crammed his mouth full, and when it was empty again he pointed to the woods and lawns around. 'Does all this belong to the College?' he asked.

'Some, not all,' the old cook said. 'Here Old George, de garden boy. Better you ask he. He tell you.'

A bent old man in khaki with a very old felt hat pulled down over his face came shambling around the corner of the kitchen. He was followed by Jacob, the young cart driver who had brought Jason to the College; and by three housemaids, Jessie, Dottie, and Maudie, all well muffled up against the morning breeze.

'Good marnin'!' each of them said to Andrew, who returned their greetings.

'You was on de ship, man?' the old gardener inquired in his deep, cracked voice.

'You bet I was,' Andrew answered, with some difficulty as his mouth was full. He hastily swallowed, as he did not want to lose his audience. His spectacles glittered. Between mouthfuls he gave a stirring account of the torpedoing of the ship, and of his escape down the side of the hull. The servants opened their mouths and eyes, and exclaimed out loud. Flattered by their attention Andrew's voice rose.

'We've lost all our clothes,' he said. 'I haven't even got a handkerchief of my own. And do you know, at New York they gave us presents. Jason got a pair of boxing gloves, and John got some music and I got a stamp album, and Pat got puzzles, and Jean and Guy got toys. But we've lost them all.'

In the midst of his tale a shutter opened above. Old Millie the nurse looked out and put her finger to her lips.

Between mouthfuls Andrew gave a stirring account of the torpedoing of the ship

'We talkin' too loud. Dat udder boy sick,' Dinah said in a low tone. 'Come, we mus' get tea ready.' She disappeared into the kitchen followed by the reluctant maids, who wanted to hear more about the ship.

'You tells it fine, man,' the old gardener said. 'Bimeby you tells we more.'

'How far does the College Beach go?' Andrew inquired of Old George.

'Come. Look over to de wes'. You see some little islands runnin' out from de shore?'

'Yes.'

'Dey is call' de Five Fishers. Dat's de end of de College Beach.'

'I see. And is it quite safe to go walking about here?'

'Safe? Where you means?'

'On the beach, or in the woods.'

'Why not?'

'I thought I'd do some exploring by myself. Are there any dangerous animals?'

'Dangerous?' Old George stared at Andrew. 'Might be a crapaud,' he said, and went away with his shoulders shaking.

Andrew decided that it might be best to take his first walk on the beach. He therefore put on his sandals, stuffed the rest of the fruit into his pockets, and ran down the steep steps past Mrs Grant's bungalow. There was no sound there. At the foot of the steps was a footpath which led through a grove to a sort of pavilion and a row of dressing-rooms. Andrew investigated these, and made a note in his new book that the pavilion was a sort of gymnasium. It had a thatched roof on pillars, and a hardwood floor raised well above the level of the beach. The dressing-rooms were for changing after swimming. He noticed that the pegs and lockers bore names of boys on school stickers.

Emerging from the shadows of the trees, Andrew felt the firm white sand under his feet. The sea was a brilliant blue with broad bands of green where the coral reef lay submerged. Between the reef and the shore was a lagoon where

the boys swam, and in the middle of it a raft was moored.
Beyond the reef fishing-boats were sailing. Except for
the far-distant boats, he might almost have been on a desert
island.

'Golly! I'm like Robinson Crusoe!' Andrew murmured.
The grove of trees hid the houses on the higher slopes, and
when Andrew had gone a few paces he could no longer see
the pavilion and the bathing cabins. The smooth white
sand was tempting. It stretched in a long crescent to the
north-west. 'Oh, boy!' Andrew said aloud; and slipped his
feet out of his sandals which he hung around his neck. For
pure joy he began to caper, and then to run at top speed a
race with his shadow. He caught it up where the beach
ended in a jumble of rocks.

'Now what's beyond this, I wonder?' Andrew asked himself. The rocks continued seaward and linked the five small
islands which George had called the Five Fishers. At high
tide they were completely cut off from one another as they
were now, and Andrew saw a strong current running
between the First Fisher and the beach.

'When I've learnt to swim,' he resolved, 'I'll go and camp
on one of those Fishers and stay all night.'

He glanced back the way he had come. There was plenty
of time to go on a little farther, he decided; so, climbing the
jumble of rocks which ended the school beach, he found
himself looking down on another bay, another half-moon
of sand even more fascinating than the last. Not a path led
through thick brushwood which fringed the sand. He
resolved to run to the end of this second beach, and see
what was beyond. The tide had just turned, and stranded
along the highwater mark were treasures too interesting to
be ignored: pink, fluted shells, black slugs, jelly-fish shining
with rainbow colours, starfish, and sea urchins.

'I'll start a collection of those things, since I've lost my
stamps,' Andrew said to himself. He ate up the fruit in his
pockets to make room for the curious things which he could
not bear to leave behind. He had no bag or handkerchief;
only his sandals, and those would not hold much. On and

on he went, and before he knew it the beach had ended in another pile of rocks. Climbing to the top of them he saw yet another beach beyond.

'There must be an end to these beaches,' Andrew murmured. 'Though if I go far enough I suppose I'll go round the whole island. But surely I haven't gone as far as that yet.' While thinking this he found himself walking briskly along this beach also, finding it just sufficiently unlike the last to be fascinating. He took out his notebook and made a little map. 'Discovery Beach,' he wrote in the bay next to College Beach. In this way he was tempted to explore two more beaches which he named Spring Beach and Gravel Beach.

By this time his pockets and hands were full, and he wished devoutly that he had something in which he could carry his treasures. He had nearly decided to take off his shirt to wrap everything up in, and return in his shorts alone, when he heard the stuttering of an outboard motor, and, looking up, saw Goldbeard's boat making through the reefs towards the shore a little farther on. At once he started to run, shouting greetings as he went. Goldbeard could not hear from that distance, and with the engine running, and Andrew soon lost sight of the boat behind another point. Here the pile of rocks which ended the beach was still higher and more difficult to climb, especially with full hands. It took Andrew some time to do it, and when he reached the top the boat was nowhere to be seen. He stared in amazement at the empty bay. A sound made him look down. The rocky pile where he stood was like a cliff on this further side, and built into the base of it was a boathouse. Goldbeard had emerged from it. The sound which Andrew had heard was of a door being slammed. Goldbeard's coat was over his arm, and from the pocket of it a newspaper dangled.

'Hi! Mr Dix!' Andrew shouted. Goldbeard turned and looked up. The expression on his face when he saw Andrew cannot easily be described. Andrew took it to be surprise. A person less friendly might have seen annoyance in it.

'Well,' Goldbeard remarked, and his voice had never

been less jovial, 'so it's you. What a way you have of turning up.' He added something under his breath that Andrew could not catch.

'Pardon?' Andrew called politely.

'What are you doing up there?'

'Exploring the island. I got up before anyone else was awake. It's super, isn't it? Is this your beach?'

'Yes. So you're exploring. You never lose yourself, do you?' Goldbeard inquired.

'Never,' Andrew said heartily. 'I notice where I'm going, and I draw a map, or put down notes. I'm a wiz at finding my way.'

'Pat turned up yet?' Goldbeard asked, after a slight pause.

'No. I think I'll go and find him, you know, like Stanley found Livingstone, because we're to have a holiday until the masters come back from their volunteering.'

'I see. Well, goodbye.' Goldbeard turned abruptly and started to walk up a footpath which led through trees up a steep slope.

'I say, can I come along?' Andrew shouted. 'I want to show you my notebook.'

'No,' said Dix with some force, and then added, 'Some other time. I'm busy now.'

When he had gone some yards up the hill Andrew noticed the newspaper drop out of the pocket of the coat which Dix still carried over his arm.

'Hi! Hi!' shouted Andrew. Goldbeard quickened his pace. 'You've dropped it, – the paper!' Andrew bawled. Goldbeard half-turned, and shouted something which Andrew did not catch, but took to mean that he didn't want it. Andrew scrambled down the side of the rocky hillock, for it occurred to him that the newspaper would be the very thing in which to wrap his treasures. He bounded up the path, and Goldbeard, seeing in a hasty glance round that he was being pursued, put on a spurt and fairly dashed up the path out of sight.

Andrew picked up the paper, rejoicing in his good luck, and carried it down to the beach again. Here, on the

'Hi, you've dropped the paper,' Andrew shouted

doorstep of the boathouse he spread it, and made a careful bundle of all his treasures. Some, of which he had more than two or three specimens, especially of the jelly-fish which seemed rather wilted, he threw away. When he had finished this, he walked around to the front of the boathouse, and peered into the dimness inside. A sort of boom had been lowered to keep the little boat from floating away. Up under the roof a larger speedboat had been raised. There was a small yacht, and a couple of rowing boats.

When he had satisfied his curiosity, Andrew debated whether to continue exploring, or whether he had better return to the College. The others would surely be up by now. He wished he had asked Goldbeard the time, and half thought of following him up to his house to do this. Then he began to think that as the sun was now very hot and high, he had better return to the college in the shelter of the trees. There was a second footpath, leading away from the boathouse back up the slope in the general direction of Badanda College, and this Andrew decided to take.

'It will be a different part to explore,' he said to himself. 'And I might find Pat.'

With a feeling of adventure, Andrew found himself going through a dense wood. He could not help glancing round over his shoulders from time to time, and looking up into the branches which hung over the path. What animals might there be in a tropical island? Might there be ratels, or armadillos, or pumas? What was that other creature of which the gardener had spoken, the crapaud? Andrew had never heard of it. He wondered if it were like a deer, or a wolf, or perhaps a sort of flying fox. He went a little quicker, listening for unusual sounds. Birds were quarrelling in the branches, but down in the shadow there seemed neither colour nor movement. No grass grew in that deep shade; there was a drab covering of dead leaves, and that was all. He began to wish that he had returned by way of the beach. Beyond this dense growth the sea was sparkling in the sunshine, under a sky of deep blue. Everything out there was light and joyful. Here it was dark and mysterious, and a trifle frightening.

Something dropped from a tree. What was it? Andrew was sure he saw a lithe body springing through the branches. He gripped his bundle hard, and ran as fast as he could along the path. When he was almost breathless he heard a sound close at hand: a heartening and unexpected sound: the clang of the College clock striking nine o'clock. Before he could stop himself he had run at top speed into the playing field of the College. There was no doubt of it. The white, arcaded buildings lay before him, placid in the sunlight. He slowed down to a walking pace, and still breathing hard, went up to a side door which the boys used. No one was about. He looked into the dining-room, and saw only empty tables. The playroom was also empty. He tiptoed up on to the top verandah and was relieved to see Miss Hall seated at a desk counting up figures.

'Good morning, Andrew,' she said in a low tone. 'Where have you been?'

'I just went out exploring,' he answered brightly.

'The servants thought you had gone down to Mrs Grant's bungalow, and we were a little anxious when we found that you weren't there. Next time take some of the other boys with you when you go exploring.'

'They were all asleep,' Andrew explained. 'I didn't know them well enough to wake them up.'

'All right. But, remember, don't go swimming by yourself.'

'I can't swim yet.'

'Even when you can, you must go with the others. The boys usually go in groups. You must be hungry.'

'Dinah gave me something to eat before I went.'

'Oh, yes. She said so. Well, you'd better go down and find out what the other boys are doing at the beach. You know there is a holiday this morning.'

'I think we should always have holidays here,' Andrew said. 'It's so hot that it's like the middle of the summer holidays all the time. It isn't right to have lessons when it's so hot.'

'You'll get used to that,' Miss Hall said. 'Run along now. Look, there's Old George taking a basket of oranges down to the beach for the boys.'

Andrew was about to obey when he remembered his bundle.

'I've got some frightfully interesting things that I picked up on the beach,' he said. 'You know, I've lost my stamp album which was in my trunk. So I've made up my mind to make a collection of beach things. I started this morning. Wouldn't you like to see them?

'Not just now ... Later on ... This evening. If they are dry you may put them into your play locker.'

'Righto! Is Jason any better?'

'About the same.'

'Have you heard anything about Pat?'

'No. They are still searching.'

'O.K.! Good-bye!' Andrew was off.

CHAPTER 8

Swimming

MRS GRANT and her children were awakened by the tapping of Jessie, bringing a tray of toast and fruit and coffee, with cocoa for the children.

'What's that?' Jean asked, pointing to the tray.

'Dis yous tea,' Jessie said, smiling good-naturedly.

'But there's no teapot,' Jean objected.

'No, but it call tea, all de same,. Miss Jean.'

'Is it our breakfast? There's no porridge.'

'Breakfast at half-pas' ten, Miss Jean.'

'And look at those teeny, little baby bananas,' Jean said. 'Why are they so small ?'

'They's figs, Miss Jean.'

'No they're not. I know what figs are. They are brown and sweet, and full of seeds. Not like this at all.'

'We does call they figs, Miss Jean.'

'I'm sure they are very nice,' Mrs Grant interposed. 'We'll get used to these strange things in time, Jessie.'

'Yes, Madam,' said Jessie giggling. 'Oh, Madam, you talk so English!' she said. They heard her laughing all the way up the steps.

'This is lovely!' Mrs Grant said when they were all sitting in the screened verandah eating the dewy melons and sweet 'figs', and enjoying the rolls and toast and jam. In spite of her criticisms, Jean also found the meal delicious. Guy wasted no time in talk, but ate all that was given him, and asked for more.

They had scarcely finished, when with suppressed laughter and undertones of talk, a swarm of boys rushed down the hill. As they got farther from the school, where they were under orders to be quiet for Jason's sake, their noise increased. They were all in bathing suits, with their clothes under their arms. Stepping leisurely after them came John, in a borrowed suit.

'Oh, Mummie, let me go and swim, too!' Jean begged.

'Darling, I can't this morning. I have no suit, and I can't leave Guy. Besides, I must go up and see about Jason.'

'Well, there's John. He'll take me. Oh, John, John! Let me go down to swim with you.'

'Jean, dear, he won't want ... No, John, why should you be bothered with her? She can stay with me.'

'I don't mind taking her,' John said good-naturedly. He did not particularly want to go down to the sea after the adventure of the day before, but he was too lazy to argue, and too good-natured to refuse the eager invitation of the boys. They were all younger than himself, and he was both shy and tired. He thought that having Jean with him might be an excuse for not being very energetic.

'It's very kind of you, John. Be a good girl, Jean. You can bathe in your sunsuit, darling. John, is there any news of Pat?'

'No.'

'I suppose you haven't seen Jason this morning?'

'No.'

'And there's no news about whether they have saved any of our luggage?'

'No.'

Mrs Grant gave a worried sigh.

'How long are you going to be at the beach?' she asked.

'We have to be back at the College at half-past ten. That's when we have breakfast.'

'Oh, yes, the maid said so. How queer. But I suppose we'll get used to these ways. Where's Andrew?'

'I don't know.'

She waved them good-bye, and John and Jean followed the boys down. When they reached the foot of the hill John saw with pleasure that the beach was shady with huge trees which grew around the pavilion. Much to the concern of the other boys he picked out a nice spot under a tree and sat down, announcing his intention to stay there.

'But you can't sit there, man,' the boys exclaimed.

'Why not?'

'Because it rained in the night, man!'

'Well, what if it did? The ground's quite dry.'

'The trees will drip on you, man!'

'I don't mind if they do,' John said, leaning comfortably against the trunk.

'But it's a manchineel tree, man!'

'What kind's that?' John asked lazily. He wondered why they did not go away to swim, and let him rest. He disliked their West Indian accent, and their way of calling him 'man' all the time.

'It's a poison tree. It'll drip on you, and you'll have blisters. Look, the little girl has got one of the fruits. Take it away from her. It's poison.'

If he had been alone John might have ignored their warnings out of sheer laziness, but he could not risk having anything happen to Jean, so he moved out of the spread of the branches and sat on the steps of the pavilion.

'Aren't you coming to swim, man?' the boys asked.

'In a few minutes,' John said, to Jean's disgust. She was too shy to go down to the water with the strange boys, and besides, she could not swim. So she sat down beside John, who was throwing pebbles at the crabs which peeped out of their holes.

The boys were disappointed, too. When Andrew had told them the tale of Guy's rescue by John, they all imagined him to be a champion. John wanted to see what they could do in the water before he showed off. He had to admit that most of them swam as well as he did, or better. These boys of Colonial families, born and bred in the tropics, were as at home in the water as on the land. They swam as naturally as they ran. Brown with the sun, their hair bleached by exposure to it, they spent their holidays dressed in swimming trunks, sailing their yachts, playing water-polo, or diving into the clear water of the lagoon. As the climate varied very little from season to season, they swam all the year round. It was a little wetter in the hot weather, and a little drier in the cooler months: that was all.

When they saw that John could not be persuaded to swim at

once they left him and started to race out to the raft. John was amazed at their speed. Their crawl was much faster than his.

'I wish I could swim,' Jean pouted.

'You'll soon learn,' John said lazily.

'I won't if no one teaches me,' Jean remarked. She sat silent for another minute, and then got up saying, 'I'm going to paddle, so there!' She took off her shoes and started to the water. John followed reluctantly. He did not particularly like to play nursemaid to a little girl. However, he need not have been self-conscious, for most of them had little sisters at home, and they took Jean's presence quite calmly.

Presently one of them, a red-headed boy named Robin Rust, came swimming back to say that there was a swimming belt in the pavilion, which could be buckled around Jean so that she could float. This he fetched, and helped John to put it round the little girl. Soon Jean was bobbing up and down and shrieking with delight. John swam lazily about. The water was so warm that he felt he could go to sleep floating on his back.

'Come out to the raft, man,' Robin urged.

'Too much fag,' John replied. 'It makes me sweat to swim in this water.'

'Come on, I'll pull the little girl,' Robin urged.

'Yes, do pull me,' Jean begged. Robin took hold of her hand and started to tow her out. John was obliged to follow. It was so pleasant that both quite forgot the horror of the preceding day. It was lovely to roll and plunge and glide through that blue-green water. The boys already on the raft held out willing hands to pull the newcomers up. Then they sat with their legs dangling and enjoyed the sun. John and Jean looked back at the shore. They saw the hillside rising behind the grove of manchineel trees, and the path climbing steeply up to Badanda College. On the top of the slope the white, arcaded buildings rose from the flowering jacaranda trees.

'I can see Mummie on the verandah of our house!' Jean shouted, and stood on the raft to wave.

For her part, Mrs Grant was amazed, and rather fright-ened to see her small daughter out on the raft among the boys. She was looking down rather helplessly when Old George came down the steps with a basket of oranges and Andrew came leaping down behind him. Andrew was dressed in borrowed bathing shorts, which were too large for his spindly shanks, and were tied up with a piece of tape.

'Good morning, Mrs Grant,' he shouted.

'Oh, Andrew,' she said. 'I see that Jean is out on the raft. I can't think how she got there. I do hope that the boys will be careful and not let her get into danger.'

'Is John there too?' Andrew asked, climbing the railing, and peering through the moonflower vines.

'Yes, there he is, lying down on the diving-board.'

'Oh, she's all right then,' Andrew cried. 'Hurrah. Oh, how perfectly mag and super!' He resumed his headlong descent, and Mrs Grant's voice came after him, 'Tell-them-to-be-careful!'

But it was all very well to rush down to the water's edge; and even to walk out as far as his armpits, but Andrew could see that in a few more steps he would be out of his depth. He flapped his arms, and gave a series of hoots calculated to let them know that he was there.

'That's Andrew splashing and shouting,' Jean said.

'Why doesn't he come out to the raft?' they asked.

'Because he can't swim,' Jean answered.

'But he can almost float in his bath,' John murmured. The boys all laughed.

'But there's another life-belt in the pavilion,' Robin said. 'I'll go back and tell him, and help him with it.'

He dived, swam for a long way under water, and came up quite near Andrew who was sitting in a foot of water persuading himself that he was floating.

'I didn't see you coming,' Andrew said with a start.

'Come out to the raft, man,' Robin urged.

'I can't quite swim yet,' Andrew explained. 'At least, not quite that far.'

D

'I'll get you a life-belt, and tow you out.'

Andrew was not as eager to trust himself to the life-belt as Jean had been.

'I'm really better on land, and climbing things, and finding my way through jungles and things,' he explained. 'Besides, my goggles get covered with water, and then I can't see to swim properly.'

'Leave them in the pavilion, man,' Robin said.

'No. Then I couldn't see at all.'

'Well, come on,' Robin urged. 'What are you waiting for, man? You can't sink with that belt on.'

'I'm just coming,' Andrew said with a nervous giggle. He could not bear to let go of a rocky point to which his toe was clinging.

'Get on, man!' Robin said, giving him a push. Then Andrew found himself floating beyond his depth, and his spirits rose to find that he did not go down like a stone.

'Here I come, everybody!' he shouted, churning along like a paddle-steamer. With enormous pride, but rather out of breath, he reached the raft at last.

'I've got a belt on too, Andrew,' Jean called.

Robin slithered up on the raft, and willing hands pulled Andrew up.

'This is super!' he exclaimed standing up on the diving-board and securing his bathing trunks which had threatened to slip off in the water. He waved his arms vigorously as a signal to Mrs Grant that he, too, had been able to get out there, and was answered by a wave of the towel.

'This is super!' he said again. 'How far out are we allowed to swim?'

'Only to the reef, by ourselves.'

'Why aren't we allowed outside?' Andrew asked, as if he were disappointed not to be allowed to swim across the Gulf of Mexico, at least.

'Currents, man, and maybe fish.'

'I'm not afraid of sharks,' Andrew said in an off-hand manner. 'I'm not usually afraid of things. I had a walk this morning through the woods, and guess what?'

'Well, what, man?'

'I was chased.'

'What chased you, man?'

'An animal,' Andrew said, 'Quite a big animal, I think. Mind you, I only saw its shadow as it sprang after me, but I think it was about the size of a fox, or a wolf, or perhaps a small tiger; and it was a brown-grey, and spotted.'

'Did it make a noise, man?' Robin asked, for the boys were staring at Andrew with round eyes.

'Yes ... At least I think I heard something,' Andrew said. 'A sort of roar, or growl. It was awfully quick, too, but I didn't run, not at first. I stood quite still, and stared right into the bushes where it was.'

John listened to this rigmarole with a contemptuous twitch of his nostrils. Why need Andrew make up stories like this? His real adventures had been exciting enough. The other boys sat goggling.

'Perhaps it was an animal out of Ginger's zoo,' someone suggested.

'Where's that?' Andrew inquired.

'Near the port. Once some of the monkeys got loose, and we caught them in the woods.'

'Oh, but this wasn't a monkey,' Andrew declared, pursing his lips and shaking his head. 'No ... Do you know what I think it was?'

'What, man?' everyone exclaimed.

'A crapaud. A wild crapaud!' Andrew said solemnly. At the same time his right eye caught the reflection of sunlight on the water, and he seemed to wink.

There was a surprised silence, and then all the boys burst into shouts of laughter. They laughed so long that Andrew, who was amazed by the reception of the story, began to laugh too.

'Oho! You fooled us well, man!' Robin shouted, throwing himself at Andrew. There was a grand free-for-all which did not end until everyone but John and Jean were struggling in the water.

Andrew came up spluttering, with a great thrashing of

arms and legs. He had swallowed pints of sea-water, but he was so relieved to feel his nose in the air again that he did not mind. His hand went up automatically to his face.

'I've lost my goggles!' he shouted. 'Hey, you fellows, I've lost my glasses!'

'Rescue the goggles!' Robin cried. He had climbed up on the raft again, but now he dived off, and swam down to the bottom. All the boys, one after the other, dived to search for the glasses. At last they were found. Andrew received them back thankfully. He was almost glad that he had lost them, as it had diverted attention from the mention of the crapaud. But the boys soon began to recall it, and could be heard chuckling, 'Chased by a wild crapaud, man!' Somehow they were all very much amused at this. Unintentionally, Andrew had gained a reputation for being a wit, or a good leg-puller. He could not make out why this was, but he wisely let the matter drop for the moment.

'Old George has brought down some oranges,' he said.

'Let's race back and eat them!' was the cry. In that grand race back to the shore Andrew was easily the last. Even John, who had taken his time, and had Jean clinging to his shoulder, passed him almost at once. Andrew struggled gamely along, using his arms like oars and kicking whenever he remembered to, and resolving grimly to learn to swim without delay.

'How long did it take you fellows to learn to swim?' he inquired when he finally joined the others on the beach. They had all learned so young that they could not remember.

'We'll teach you. You'll soon learn, man,' Robin comforted him. Robin had taken a great liking to Andrew, and his two special friends, Jack, a fat, smiling boy, and Bruce, a flaxen-haired boy of about Andrew's height, followed his lead. Andrew expanded in the warmth of this friendliness. The newcomers were told the rules of the beach.

'We can't go swimming alone,' Robin said.

'And we can only sail our boats inside the lagoon unless the boatmen go with us. Sometimes in good weather we go right past the port to the Yacht Club.'

'We three have a rowing boat,' Bruce said to Andrew. 'At least, we will have it when it's finished. We're working on it.'

'How super!' Andrew exclaimed. 'I wish I could help.'

'Better learn to swim first,' John remarked quietly.

At this point Robin gave a certain signal to Bruce and Jack, and both boys got up and followed him a short way down the beach where they put their heads together and whispered earnestly. A silence fell upon the others. Andrew said suddenly;

'Look at that queer old chap coming along.'

They all turned.

'It's Mr Solomon,' they exclaimed.

'Good old Sollyollyman!' Robin murmured. He had returned with his friends to the others.

The person who was approaching was an old negro with very black skin and white woolly hair, a dignified figure though dresssed rather quaintly in a high, stiff collar, a sort of alpaca frock coat, a white waistcoat and trousers, and a white panama hat. He wore a pair of white-rimmed sun-glasses which made odd rings in his black face. He spoke carefully, in clear, precise tones.

'*Salvete,* boys,' he called to them, 'You have been learning, I conjecture, to conjugate the verb *natare*, to swim. Learn it well. Here I see are two newcomers who have hardly even begun to learn it, being still upheld by life-belts. Do not use the cribs too long, I counsel you, or you will not learn to swim alone.'

Andrew and Jean, to whom he spoke, fingered their belts and were a little mystified. The other boys jostled affectionately around Mr Solomon.

'What about the examination?' they cried. 'Who came first?'

'You will be told in due course,' he replied wagging his head. 'Wait until class time.'

'But it's a holiday, Mr Solomon, because of the fire in the town.'

'All the masters are in the volunteers, Mr Solomon.'

'Ah! Then we will construe the little sentence, "It's an ill wind that blows no one any good".'

A bell rang from the top of the hill.

'Breakfast!' was the general cry. The boys jumped up, and dashed off to change in the bathing huts behind the pavilion.

'You go on up the steps, Jean,' John said. 'You've got to go home to change.'

'Come with me, little girl,' Mr Solomon said.

Jean followed him shyly. He had a kind smile, and the boys liked him, but she had not seen black people before, and did not want to take his hand.

Seeing that she was well on her way up the steps, and that Mrs Grant was looking over the verandah of her bungalow, John followed the other boys into the changing rooms. Some of them were already changed, and were charging up the hill. John heard Andrew ask,

'Who is that old man?' and Robin reply, 'Old Solomon? He teaches us while Mr Popham is away.'

'Who is Mr Popham?'

'He's our regular master, but he's gone to join the R.A.F. Mr Boomhill asked Mr Solomon to come until we can get someone else. He's retired, really. He used to be head of a coloured school.'

'I see,' said Andrew. 'You ready, Robin? I'll beat you up the steps.'

But when Robin, breathless with victory, turned round to crow over his new friend, Andrew was nowhere to be seen. On his upward scramble after Robin he had caught sight of Old George washing his hands under the tap behind the kitchen, and wishing to clear up things in his mind, he swerved off the path to the left, ran between the bushes until he was no longer in danger of being seen if Robin should turn.

'George!' Andrew said in a breathless, confidential whisper, 'what is a crapaud?'

'A crapaud, man?' George said, with a sidelong look, and a half smile on his wrinkled old face. 'You wants to know what a crapaud is? Come, I show you a crapaud.' He took

'What about the examination, Mr Solomon?'

Andrew by the shoulder and directed him to the gutter which ran behind the kitchen. 'See,' he said, pointing, 'That a crapaud.'

'But ... But I don't see anything there but a toad,' Andrew said.

'A toad ... dat a crapaud,' Old George said.

CHAPTER 9

Pat is Found

BEFORE 'breakfast' it was Mr Boomhill's custom to take prayers in the Hall, and he was standing with his Bible in his hand when Andrew, considerably dashed in his mind, entered. Robin, who had been looking for him everywhere, pounced on him.

'I want to speak to you after breakfast,' he said in a whisper. Jack and Bruce, who were close to Robin as usual, beamed as if they shared the important secret which Robin was to communicate. Andrew hoped that they did not mean to penalize him for the way he had behaved in the morning. He was glad, therefore, that there was no opportunity for talk just then. For once, he had little to say, though there might be much to explain.

Mr Boomhill and Mr Jones, who stood behind him, had been out all night helping to put out the fire, and they both looked rather tired. Mr Boomhill seemed quite shocked that such events could happen in his well-ordered life. Mrs Grant came up with her two children, and was conducted to a seat near Miss Hall. Andrew was interested to see a car drive up and Goldbeard, seeing that prayers were about to begin, hesitated a moment, then came up, and nodding to Mr Boomhill, took a seat at the back. Last of all Mr Solomon, with a sheaf of papers under his arm, hung up his panama and came towards the seat he usually occupied. When he passed the school clock he stopped and, taking out his watch, shook his head as he compared them.

'Good morning, Mr Solomon,' said Mr Boomhill, with the slightest hint of impatience.

'Good morning, sir. I take the liberty of thinking that the school clock is fast by nearly four minutes.'

'What makes you think so?' Mr Boomhill asked. He raised his white bushy eyebrows and his whole scalp slid forward over his head to meet them. This was his way of signifying displeasure, and the boys always watched the contortion with interest.

'I have no less authority, sir, than Big Ben himself, with which I set my watch this morning.'

'Big Ben?' echoed Mr Boomhill. 'But I thought that your wireless was out of order.'

'And that no one on the island could repair it,' added Mr Jones, trying to raise his eyebrows like his superior.

'So it was, so it was,' chuckled the old man, his black face wrinkling up into a thousand pleased creases. 'But it has been restored to working order, Mr Boomhill and Mr Jones, by the most extraordinary and unexpected visitor we ever had.' He paused, with his head on one side, looking around at the roomful of attentive people. 'Yesterday,' he said, 'I was away from home all day, endeavouring to assist some of my old relatives who were involved in the lamentable occurrences in the town. There being no buses, as you know, I was forced to return all the way home on foot, and did not arrive there until after dark. You will never guess what I found there.' He paused, but no one spoke. He looked around with a pleased smile at the expectant faces. 'I found,' he said in his precise way, 'a child, a white boy about eight years old, sleeping peacefully in my house, and I ask you to believe that this unknown child had done what the radio experts on the island could not accomplish. He had made the radio work.'

'Pat!' Goldbeard shouted.

'Could it be Pat?' Mrs Grant exclaimed at the same time.

'Of course it's old Patrick, the machine wiz!' squeaked Andrew.

'It must be our missing scholar!' cried Mr Boomhill. 'One of the survivors taken from the ship, who has been missing ever since.'

'*Mirabile dictu!*' smiled Mr Solomon. 'And here was I, on the point of asking you to allow me to take the time off to report the case to the authorities. I assure you, he is the most extraordinary child.'

'Didn't he tell you his name?' Mr Boomhill asked.

'No, he would not. I thought at first that he was deaf and dumb, for when I asked his name, and where he had come from, and where he was going, he would not answer. My mother told me about a big boy, or young man, who had carried him in, and who had said that he would return. We kept watching for him but he did not come back, and finally we decided to report the presence of the child in our house.'

'The older boy was hurt, and has been ill. In fact he has been unconscious here, and therefore unable to tell us what he had done with the little boy,' Mr Boomhill explained.

'Well, well,' Mr Solomon said. 'I assure you again that this child, this Patrick, is a most extraordinary child. He not only repaired the radio, but reconditioned a mousetrap, and unlocked a trunk of which we had lost the key. The members of my family, or all of them who have returned home to rest after yesterday's frightful events, have taken a great fancy to him. My mother, I think, considers him a sort of celestial visitor. Ha! ha!' His face creased again into its many, benevolent wrinkles.

'Why did you not bring him with you?' asked Mr Boomhill. 'After all, even if we had had no claim on him, it would have been a natural thing for us to take care of a boy like that.'

'It was too late last night, and I had no one to send. This morning I did think of it, but the child would not come. He shook his head at all my suggestions that he should go from the house. Finally I left him mending a toy for little Joseph.'

'We must go and get him immediately,' Mrs Grant exclaimed.

'I'll go with you!' shouted Andrew radiantly.

'I think not,' Mrs Grant said. 'I had better take Guy, as he may not want to stay here without me, and I will take Jean as she is a great friend of Pat's, and he might be more willing to come with her.'

'Is ... Is the child quite well?' Dix asked suddenly. He had not come forward, but had repeatedly wiped his face and neck with his handkerchief as if overcome with the heat.

'He is sound in wind and limb, and in mind,' Mr Solomon said, turning in his direction.

'I must go at once,' Mrs Grant said.

'Won't you wait until after breakfast?' Miss Hall asked.

'No, no. I can't wait. I must bring him back. He was in my care, you know, and I have been so dreadfully worried.'

'I will put on my hat and accompany you,' Mr Solomon said. 'Dear me, Mammy and Joseph and the others will be very sorry to see him go. Well, well, so this unknown child is to be one of my own pupils!' He laughed again.

'I'll take you in the car,' Mr Jones said. He had not volunteered his services at first, but had tried to catch Mr Boomhill's eye, and Mr Boomhill had looked at Mr Dix with clear meaning, while Dix lit a cigarette and looked at no one.

'You will excuse us if we do not delay,' Mrs Grant said, taking Jean and Guy to the front steps.

'Yes, go, by all means,' Mr Boomhill replied, throwing a vexed, sidelong look at Mr Dix, whose car stood ready in the drive. 'And, meanwhile,' he went on, raising his voice a little, 'we will have prayers, and start breakfast.'

Dix retired discreetly with his cigarette. He helped Mrs Grant and the children into the car, but did not offer to go with them. As the boys' voices rose in a hymn, he lingered out of sight on the front porch looking from time to time down the avenue along which the car had vanished. Prayers were soon over, and the sound of chairs being moved and feet scraping indicated that the boys were entering the dining-room. Mr Boomhill did not go to his breakfast, but came out to the porch. Andrew, who had followed him in order to watch for the return of Mrs Grant, heard Dix say, 'I think it would be as well for there to be no fuss when the child arrives.'

'I think you may safely leave that to me,' Mr Boomhill replied.

'I beg your pardon,' Dix laughed. 'I must appear foolish. I mean, as we have all been so disturbed.'

'You may remember,' Mr Boomhill said coldly, 'I did

not share your anxiety about him, beyond a natural vexation that he was not enjoying the comforts of the College. I knew that he must have taken shelter somewhere, and would be returned to us safe and sound.'

'You were quite right,' Dix agreed heartily. 'I confess that I must have behaved rather foolishly. You have had to deal with boys in such numbers that, of course, your judgement of them would be far sounder than mine.'

'In my thirty years of school teaching,' Mr Boomhill said, and he sounded slightly mollified, 'I have had considerable experience. Well, here they are.'

Andrew dashed off on tiptoe, and found John placidly sitting at table, waiting with the others for his meal.

'Come, John,' he said. 'The car's back.'

'Well?' John said.

'Well, come!'

'Did anyone ask for me?' John asked.

'No, but of course you must come to meet him.'

'What is the matter, Andrew?' Miss Hall asked. She had been pouring out coffee.

'Pat's back,' Andrew explained. In order not to keep up the argument John asked permission to leave, and followed Andrew on to the porch, and Miss Hall and many of the boys came out, too.

When Pat came up the steps with Mrs Grant you could not have told from his expression that he had gone through any unusual experience. He did not look up at Mr Boomhill who stood with his hands out and a welcoming smile on his face.

'Well, well!' the Headmaster said heartily, 'So you have arrived at last, my boy.'

'Say good morning, Pat,' Mrs Grant urged.

'Good morning,' Pat replied obediently.

'Say good morning, Mr Boomhill, and shake hands,' whispered Mrs Grant.

'Good morning Mr Boom,' Pat said, putting up his hand, but looking straight ahead. There was a burst of giggling from the boys.

'Now for breakfast,' Mr Boomhill said briskly. 'We are all here now, and all hungry.'

'Pat has had breakfast,' Mr Jones said. 'The old lady saw to that. She was quite affected when she said "good-bye" to him.'

'Then Pat can come here and sit down and look at the books on this table until we have finished our meal,' Mr Boomhill said. 'We won't be long, my boy.'

'I'll let him look at my collection,' Andrew exclaimed.

'So you have started a collection already?' Dix asked. He had come in and taken a seat near Pat.

'By the way,' Mr Boomhill inquired of Dix as Andrew dashed into the playroom to get his bundle, 'did you want to see me about anything in particular this morning?'

'I just wanted to ask about Jason, and to see if Pat had turned up. And I wanted a word with young Andrew,' said Dix.

'Here's my collection,' Andrew panted. He placed the damp bundle in the Headmaster's hands.

'But what is this?' Mr Boomhill said, holding it out and looking at it in great distaste.

'You see, my stamp album was lost in my luggage on board,' Andrew explained. 'So I made up my mind to start a new one. So I am going to collect seaweed and shells and things that one finds on beaches. I picked up your paper to wrap them in,' Andrew went on looking at Dix. 'I shouted to tell you that you'd dropped it, and I thought you wouldn't mind my using it, because I had nothing else to wrap my things in.'

Mr Boomhill had been turning the parcel about gingerly, but suddenly his eyes fell upon the date, and he gave a start.

'What's this?' he said in an astonished tone, 'this is a Trinidad paper of yesterday's date. How on earth did you get hold of this?'

As he spoke he tried to straighten out the sheet to get a better view of the date, and the whole collection which Andrew had brought dropped upon the verandah with a wet thud.

'It's one that Mr Dix dropped this morning, but I didn't think he wanted it,' Andrew said, going on his knees to try to recover his treasures. Pat, sitting on the edge of a chair, looked at the scattered collection calmly.

'Mr Dix dropped it this morning?' Boomhill exclaimed. 'What do you mean?'

'Well, this morning I went for an early walk, to explore,' Andrew said brightly, 'and I saw Mr Dix coming in with his speedboat. So I ran along and saw him at his boathouse. Then, when he walked up the hill, this paper fell out of his pocket. I called after you, to tell you,' he said to Dix. 'But you shouted something back, and I thought you meant that I could have it.'

'As a matter of fact,' Dix said, 'I didn't quite know what it was you shouted, and I didn't miss the paper until I got up to the house. Then I went back, and found it gone. So I came over to see if by any chance you had picked it up, because I rather wanted it.' He held out his hand.

'Wait a moment,' said Mr Boomhill. 'This needs some explanation. To my certain knowledge there has been no boat or plane in from Trinidad for these three days. How, then, do you come to be in possession of a Trinidad paper bearing yesterday's date? Will you explain.'

Dix leaned closer and took the paper out of Boomhill's hands.

'Sorry,' he said. 'I'm rather pressed for time just now. Thank you so much. Good-bye, sir. Good-bye, Pat. See you again, Andrew. Don't let me keep you from breakfast.'

CHAPTER 10

The Secret Band

As Dix walked away, Mr Boomhill took an involuntary step forward and planted his foot squarely down on Andrew's collection. One of the jelly-fish burst with a loud pop.

Mr Boomhill jumped. For an instant he glared as if about to kick the collection off the verandah, then he took a deep breath, and made a visible effort to control his temper. He watched Goldbeard's car disappearing down the avenue with a long, baffled look, then said,

'Throw that rubbish away, boy, and come to breakfast.' He stalked towards the dining-room scowling darkly. With his rather long arms and heavy shoulders Andrew thought he looked very like a bear, and that it might be wise just now to keep out of his way. What should he do with his precious collection? Pat sat there stolidly looking at it.

'Do you want to play with these things, Pat?' Andrew asked in a low tone.

'No,' said Pat frankly.

Miss Hall came out to see why Andrew did not come in to breakfast.

'I don't know what to put these things in,' Andrew explained. 'It's my collection.'

'But why on earth did you put them in the middle of the floor?' Miss Hall asked.

'They dropped out of the paper when Mr Boomhill opened it,' Andrew explained. Miss Hall made a sound of impatience.

'Well, go and get one of those wicker trays from the table on the back verandah,' she said at last, 'and put them out there until you can arrange them properly. Some of them you can't keep, because they will smell. Mr Jones will tell you about the best way to deal with them. Now, hurry up. Wash your hands before you go in.'

As Andrew sped out to the verandah to get the wicker tray Dr Thorne's car drove up. 'There's the doctor to see Jason,' Miss Hall said. 'Come, Pat, we'll go upstairs with him, and I'll show you where you're to sleep and keep your things.'

Pat rose obediently, took Miss Hall's hand as she greeted the doctor, and went upstairs with her and Dr Thorne.

'Another new boy, surely,' remarked the doctor.

'Yes, the one that was missing. It seems that Jason took him to Mr Solomon's house, and he has been there all night. I think perhaps you'd better look at him, to see if he is any the worse for his experiences on the ship.'

Pat was quite friendly with the doctor. He asked to listen to his own heart with the stethoscope, and examined the doctor's bag with interest. He remained quietly on the verandah while the doctor and Miss Hall were in Jason's room, and then went downstairs with them.

'Come and have a cup of coffee with us,' Miss Hall suggested.

'Yes, I will,' Dr Thorne replied.

When they entered the dining-room Andrew had just finished a large plate of turtle soup, and was looking with astonished eyes at the second course of this 'breakfast', which was a highly spiced stew with a generous helping of fried yams and salad.

'Mummie, I can't eat any more. Let me go and play with Pat,' Jean said.

'Will you excuse her?' Mrs Grant asked. 'She is not used to so large a meal at this time in the morning.'

'Certainly, certainly,' Mr Boomhill said. 'She must get used to our ways, but we will let her learn gradually. Out you go.'

'You can play with my collection,' Andrew called out. 'My goodness,' he added to Robin. 'I've never seen such a breakfast as this. It is what I would call a dinner.'

Mr Boomhill looked at Mr Jones, and his eyebrows rose and his scalp moved forward balefully. Mr Jones pursed his lips and shook his head at Andrew who did not see him, and went straight on.

'First soup, "turtle, green and glutinous", and the first time I've eaten it; and then meat. I suppose we'll even have pud . . .' John saw Mr Jones' expression, and gave Andrew a sharp kick under the table.

'Ow!' Andrew yelled. 'I beg your pardon, sir, but some-one kicked me. John, why did you kick me? It was you, I'm sure!'

John gave up.

'We don't usually talk quite so much at table,' said Mr Jones, stretching his long neck up. 'We usually eat quietly, and then do our talking outside. We're to have a holiday to-day, so there will be plenty of time later for conversation.' He gave Andrew an encouraging nod.

Dr Thorne meanwhile had sat down on Mr Boomhill's right.

'There are some disturbing rumours running about,' he remarked. 'I hear strangers have been seen on the more isolated beaches. One of them is even said to have shot at a fisherman.'

'The enemy has shown himself so impudent that we must take more precautions than we have done,' Mr Boomhill said. 'We must keep on the alert. Let watchfulness be our slogan.'

'I had a look at the boy Pat,' the doctor went on. 'He seems quite fit.'

'Thank Heaven for that,' Mrs Grant said. 'It was really providential the way that Jason took the child to Mr Solomon's house. By the way, how is Jason? Or haven't you seen him?'

'Yes, I have seen him. He seems much the same. It was a considerable distance for him to carry the child. Must have been a great strain.'

'When I went for him this morning,' Mrs Grant said, 'I found Pat eating fried fish and sweet potatoes as if he had always lived there. The old woman did not wish to let him go. She kept calling him an angel.'

'She's quite a wonderful old woman,' the doctor said.

'Can she really be Mr Solomon's mother?'

'I believe so.'

'But he must be over seventy.'

'She is well over ninety. She was born a slave, I believe, but though she never learned to read herself, she was determined that her son should go to school. She begged books for him, and somehow or other had him taught. He had a sort of natural instinct for learning.'

'Yes, that is so,' said Mr Boomhill, who had now nearly recovered his serenity. 'As a matter of fact when he was a boy he attracted the attention of the bishop who sent him to England to school. When he came back he became a teacher amongst his own people. Since his retirement he has been kept busy with private pupils. When Mr Popham left us to join the R.A.F. I considered myself fortunate to be able to get him to fill the place for a few hours a day.'

The boys, who had all heard this story a score of times, began talking amongst themselves again, and Robin whispered to Andrew:

'As soon as breakfast is over, I want to say something to you. It's very special.'

'All right,' Andrew returned in the same conspiratorial whisper. 'And I have to get my collection from the back verandah.'

'Collection of what?'

'Of shells and things. I picked them up on the beach this morning.'

A hush fell. Mr Boomhill was rising and putting back his chair. This was a signal that everyone should do the same. Andrew was not sorry, as he felt that he could eat no more.

After grace had been said, the boys poured out to enjoy their holiday. Mr Boomhill and Mr Jones retired to their rooms to rest after their sleepless night, and the boys were enjoined to go down to the beach if they wanted to make a noise, or to read quietly if they stayed in the playroom.

'Come with me,' Robin said, seizing Andrew's arm.

'First let me get my collection.' Andrew sought for his tray, and the two boys started off round the kitchen. Jessie the maid met them.

'Where you is goin' wit dat tray, man?' she asked.

'Nowhere.'

'Yes you is! Come, put it down! It a breakfas' tray!'

'O, Jessie,' Andrew said. 'I want to start a museum with these things and I haven't anywhere to put them. Look at them, aren't they lovely?'

Jessie threw up her hands and laughed uproariously.

'Dinah,' she called, 'come see things is so lovely!'

Dinah came to the door, and grinned at the collection of slugs and shells and pebbles spread out on the tray.

'I had a beautiful jelly-fish,' Andrew said, 'It was like a rainbow, all kinds of colours. But Mr Boomhill stepped on it, and it popped.' Both servants shrieked with laughter for so long that Andrew thought they would never stop. Finally Dinah wiped her eyes and said, 'Here a tin box for yous tings.'

'Thank you, Dinah,' Andrew piped. 'And can I leave them with you until I have time to see Mr Jones about them? He's going to show me how to fix them so that they won't smell.'

'Oh laws, man,' she chuckled. 'They safe with we. We not wantin' any of them, man.'

'Oh, thanks awfully,' said Andrew, with touching gratitude. 'It's extremely kind of you.'

'Oho! You a little friend to me, eh?' Dinah exclaimed, and the servants laughed again, and the boys could hear them laughing as they went up the hill.

Beyond the shrubbery the bare summit of the hill stuck up above the tree-tops. Ages ago, this high straight edge of coral cliff had been a beach, but some earthquake below the sea had thrust the whole island up, and formed more dry land round it. From the edge the hill sloped sharply down to the present beach, and the hillside was thickly covered with trees whose leaves through thousands of years had fallen and decayed and mixed with coral and sand to form soil. Above the trees, the hillside was covered with scrub, and goats and sheep had worn little mazy tracks here and there. Robin suddenly struck off into one of these tracks, went around a bush, dived through another, and disappeared. Andrew, following closely, stopped and looked around amazed to find himself alone. A stifled giggling reassured him, and thrusting aside some thick foliage, he found himself in a smooth grassy hollow completely shut out from the world.

'Hail, brother,' Robin said, with both hands raised.

'Hail, brother!' Jack and Bruce echoed, with the same gesture.

Andrew grinned happily.

'We want you to be in our Secret Band,' Robin explained.

'Oh! Thanks.'

'Will you swear not to tell anyone about our secrets?'

'You bet I will. I mean you bet I won't!' Andrew said fervently.

'And you won't betray our hiding place?'

'Never!'

'Cross your heart and hope to be eaten by sharks?' Robin insisted.

'I do.'

'Then stand on your head and swear.'

With a good deal of laughter the boys helped Andrew to balance on his head, in which position he repeated their magic words. He was then placed right side up, and instructed to eat a lollipop and sing a song at the same time. This Andrew did without any great difficulty, as his mouth was capacious beyond most.

This ceremony of initiation over, they proceeded to tell him how to behave when he was one of their band of brothers.

'I pass the word when to come here,' Robin said. 'You must never let anyone follow you. The other kids are always trying to find out where we go. Now that you are one of the Secret Four they'll try to get at you. Always come here by one of our ways, where you can look back at least three points to see if you are being followed.'

'It's jolly nice,' Andrew said. 'It's a fine place. I'm not sure that I could find it again.'

'We'll teach you the way,' Jack said. 'And if you do miss it, we have our secret call, like a keskidee bird, and we'll answer you.'

'Now let's get to business,' Bruce said.

Business, apparently, was kept in a flat tin box which was deposited for safety in a hole which had been dug out of the turf. It was covered by a flat stone which was concealed by a branch of dead furze. In the box was kept a supply of lollipops to which all contributed. There were also pencils and papers, a wad of comics which were not allowed in the school as Mr Boomhill called them trash. There was also a spyglass of antique make which they had converted into a periscope by means of a couple of mirrors so that they could survey the surrounding country and see if anyone was approaching outside their sheltering bushes.

'I think this is super,' Andrew said. 'Thanks awfully for letting me be one of the Secret Four.'

'You see,' Robin explained, 'Tom White used to be the Fourth of the Secret Band, but since he left we have been one short. That's why we let you in.'

'What happened to him?' Andrew asked, wondering if Tom had sacrificed his life in this cause.'

'He went to a school in Venezuela,' Jack explained. 'Why?'

'His family moved there. He didn't want to go. Our school is the best in the West Indies,' Bruce said.

'Of course it is,' Andrew exclaimed.

'Of course we four always stick up for each other,' Robin said.

'To the death!' Andrew cried fervently.

'Sometimes we play a sort of game, like Treasure Island, or Kidnapped, or something,' Robin said. 'Just now we haven't anything on hand. We'll have to start a new one.'

'Well, you all heard what Dr Thorne said this morning,' Bruce said.

'About strangers who have been seen upon the beaches?' asked Robin.

'Yes. And one of them shot at a fisherman. I vote that we keep our eyes open, and do some sleuthing.'

Andrew opened his mouth to say something, but he closed it again, so abruptly that he bit his tongue. For once in his life he did not say at once what was in his mind.

CHAPTER 11

What Really Happened

ON the third day after his arrival at Badanda College, Jason regained consciousness. He was astonished to find himself in a bed. He did not at first remember leaving the ship, and wondered why he was not in the narrow cabin. The room seemed very large. An unfamiliar voice came from somewhere. With an effort he turned his head and saw Old Millie in her white cap and apron sitting by the window reading hymns to herself in a low drone. The memory of the calamity, the rescue of Pat, and the long, hot walk in the sun came little by little back to him. He began to think that he must be in the hut where he had left Pat, and that Millie was the old grandmammie. The bed in which he lay, however, was certainly not the enormous, pink-curtained one in which the old woman had been lying. It was a small white one. There was no bead curtain hanging before the door. A white table at his side held a collection of glasses and bottles, and there was a temperature chart hanging on the wall.

'I'm in a hospital,' Jason said to himself. 'Someone has picked me up. I wonder where the others are, and if they got off the boat. I'd better find out.' He tried to call 'Nurse!' but though his lips moved, at first no sound came. He waited for a moment, and then tried again. This time he made a faint whisper, but the old woman was turning a page of her hymn-book, and did not hear it. The third attempt drew her attention, however. Looking up, she saw that he was conscious.

'Praise de Lawd, man,' she said. 'You done woke up, eh?' She came over and put her hand on his. 'You likes a drink, man, eh?' she asked, and when Jason nodded she gently raised his head and gave him some orange juice to sip. It was delicious. 'Now I must call Miss Hall,' she said. Who

Miss Hall could be Jason had no idea, but she was close at hand, for it was not more than a couple of minutes before she came in.

'Am I in hospital?' Jason asked.

'Yes, in the College infirmary,' she answered.

Jason lay and puzzled over this for a few minutes. Then he said:

'I suppose the man brought me here in his cart?'

'Yes, he did. He is one of the gardeners. Don't talk too much. I've sent for Mrs Grant. She will be so glad that you are better. Ah! here she is.'

'Well, Jason, you have been ill!' Mrs Grant said. 'How do you feel?'

'All right,' he answered weakly. 'You all got off the ship safely?'

'Yes, we are all safe,' Mrs Grant assured him. 'Pat, too. Would you like to see him?'

'Not particularly,' said Jason. 'Where's John?'

'He's downstairs. When the doctor comes we'll ask him if John can come up to see you.'

'What day is this?' he next asked.

'Monday.' He looked puzzled. 'You've been ill for three days,' Miss Hall said. 'But you'll soon be quite well again. The boys will be so glad to hear that you are better. They are longing to see you.'

'More than I'm longing to see them,' Jason thought, closing his eyes because he did not want to speak any more. He felt very weak and stiff, and the idea of having to face more than a hundred inquisitive, strange boys did not at all appeal to him. He was thankful when the doctor advised that he be kept quiet for a day or so before even John was admitted.

Mr Boomhill came, of course, with Mr Jones, to visit Jason as soon as he heard that he had regained consciousness.

'Well, my boy,' he said in a tone which was meant to be kind, 'so you are on your way to recovery. You will be well cared for. Have you everything you wish?'

'Yes, thank you,' said Jason.

'Your father and I were schoolfellows,' Mr Boomhill continued. 'I expect that he has told you of some of the pranks we played together. Well, well, that's ancient history, eh? You are quite like him. Make haste and get well. There are jolly times ahead. We are all looking forward to the day when you will take your place amongst us.'

Jason disliked Mr Boomhill at sight

Jason closed his eyes. He disliked Mr Boomhill at sight. He could scarcely believe that his father had ever been a close friend of his. He must have changed a great deal. He could easily imagine his father a boy, for he had seen pictures of him from the time he was a baby; but Mr Boomhill, with his ponderous, stiff body, his grey-curly head and bushy moustache and eyebrows, and his emphatic voice seemed one of those people who have never been young. He did not like Mr Jones either. More than ever he felt aggrieved that he had been sent away from his English school.

Jason recovered rapidly, and at last the day came when the doctor said that John could come and see him.

Both boys were rather shy at first. Jason was still weak, and was furious to find himself feeling tearful whenever he sat up for long. John didn't know what to talk about. He tiptoed in rather shyly, and was shocked to see Jason so white under the bandage which was wound round his head.

'Hello, Jass Old Son,' he said, trying to talk in his usual way. 'You do look rather like a convict with that hair cut!'

'They shaved it because of this stupid cut.'

John sat down shyly, and there was a moment of silence. Then Jason asked:

'What sort of a place is this College?'

'Not bad,' John told him.

'Pretty loathsome, I'd say from what I've seen of it!'

'But you haven't seen much yet, have you?'

'I've seen old Boomerang. He's enough in himself! And then that awful Jones person.'

'Oh, they're not too bad, really.' John refused to look on the black side.

'What other masters are there?'

'Well, most of the Staff seem to have gone into the Forces, the younger ones at least. There seem to be some temporary and some part-time people. Two of them used to teach here, and had retired. They come in every day. Then the Bishop comes for Scripture, and special Maths and Science men come so many times a week. It's a make-shift sort of arrangement, but they're all right. You can't blame the school.'

Jason was silent. John knew all about the place already. He had met the boys and masters. It would have been more bearable if they had gone into it together and could have talked over first impressions, as they had done on board ship.

'Was anything saved of our luggage?' he asked after a time.

'Not much, a wooden box full of Mrs Grant's books,' John said. 'But I believe that they salvaged quite a lot of cargo. All our clothes and things are gone though.'

'So my boxing-gloves are gone, too,' Jason remarked.

'Afraid so, everything.'

'And what are we going to wear?'

'They've sent us all we need.'

'Who do you mean by "they"?'

'Lady May and her committee.'

'Who is Lady May?'

'Oh, of course, you weren't with us. Well, all of us survivors had to go to a sort of emergency centre where they
had food and bundles of clothes and things. And they took
notes of what we needed, and those whose clothes were
torn or wet had to be fitted out at once . . .'

'We are refugees, aren't we?' Jason said, with a bitter
laugh. 'How did you manage to get on shore?'

'I swam along, you know, and afterwards Old Dix came
in a speedboat and took us across to the wharf. All the
buildings were blazing.'

'Yes, I saw that. That's why I went the other way.'

'The fire spread through a lot of the town,' John said.
'The masters were with the volunteers fighting it. They've
only just got it under control, and we've begun classes. We
had holidays for two days.'

'What's the dorm like?'

'Quite decent. There are only four in ours. You and I
are the oldest.'

'Not Andrew, I hope.'

'No. He's with a mob in a big dorm.'

'Something to be thankful for,' Jason said.

'He's learning to swim,' John said. 'By the way, Jason,
the swimming is first class. And there's sailing. I wish we
could get hold of a sailing-boat. Lots of the boys have their
own. They build them.'

'That would be rather fun,' Jason agreed. Anything to do
with the sea was all right with Jason.

Miss Hall came in to warn John that he must go.

'To-morrow you will be able to come again for a little
longer,' she promised.

But when John came, the next day, he carried an
enormous book.

'What on earth's that?' Jason wanted to know.

'Some organ music.'

'I thought you said you'd lost all your music.'

'So I have. This isn't mine. It belongs to Lady May. She asked me to play at St George's Church as the organist is away. I've promised to go this afternoon and try the organ.'

'You would!' Jason remarked in disgust. 'I suppose you'll always be playing when I want you to do anything with me.'

'Don't be a nitwit, Jass old son,' John said, looking uneasily at his friend. Jason was so weak that the tears were always ready to start to his eyes, and this made him angry with himself. He was almost relieved when Miss Hall interrupted them by saying:

'Here are other visitors to see you, Jason. An old friend and a new one. John, perhaps you had better go now. You can come again to-morrow.'

Jason was delighted to see Goldbeard Dix, radiant in white linen, with his hair and beard like molten gold.

'Well, Jason,' he said, 'here you are. Feeling better, eh? Lady May, allow me to present my friend Jason Foster.'

'So you're the missing hero,' Lady May beamed. 'I've heard all about you. You must get better as fast as you can. It's a waste of time to be ill in Tripadoes. There are so many gorgeous things to do. You like games, don't you?'

'Yes, rather!' said Jason, rather overwhelmed.

'You must come along to see me with your friend John, the musician.'

'Jason is interested in the navy,' Dix said.

'Of course he is. Who isn't?' Lady May smiled.

'I've got a small yacht,' Dix went on. 'It needs a bit of overhauling. I thought I'd sail it round into the school lagoon. If you'd lend a hand in overhauling it, I could teach you how to sail.'

'That would be marvellous!' Jason said.

'And later on you and I and John can do a bit of navigating around the island, if Mr Boomhill will agree.'

'I'm sure Mr Boomhill will be delighted!' Lady May exclaimed.

'Good afternoon, Lady May,' said another voice. 'And what is it that I will be delighted to do? Any service to you, of course, would delight me.'

It was the Headmaster.

'Good afternoon, Mr Boomhill,' said the Governor's wife. 'Mr Dix was just saying that Jason wanted to go into the navy; and he was telling him that he had a small yacht which the boys could learn to sail. I said that I was sure you would give your permission, as you yourself are so fond of yachting.'

'Ah, yes, yes, yes! It depends on circumstances, of course,' Mr Boomhill said, darting a curious look at Goldbeard who still smiled as if he were pleased with all the world.

Lady May continued her bright chat for a few minutes. Jason scarcely heard what she said. He was interested in watching Mr Boomhill who seemed in turn to be watching Dix covertly. The Headmaster made constant efforts to tear his eyes away from the visitor, but in a moment his glance would go stealing back and he would look at him as if in fascination mixed with fear. Dix acted as if he were quite unaware of this. He laughed and joked in his usual way, and Lady May seemed to regard him like a younger brother. Mr Boomhill's eyebrows went up and up, and his scalp moved forward until it looked as though it would come loose. Jason determined to stick by Dix in spite of the Headmaster's dislike.

Mr Boomhill hung around, as Jason thought, unwilling not to stay as long as Lady May was there, and yet unable to be natural with Dix. Jason was not sorry when they all left.

Dr Thorne, who followed, was the only one to realize how weak Jason felt at first.

'Don't urge him to do things,' he said to Miss Hall. 'Let him get better slowly. Get him out on the top verandah in a long chair, and let him walk about up there if he wishes. Keep the mob away from him.'

This was easier to say than to do. The news of Jason's recovery was quick to spread. Strange, grinning faces were always appearing around the doors, and friendly hands waved to him from a distance. Offerings were even left if Old Millie were not at her post. The top verandah, however, was a pleasant place for a convalescent. One could lie and watch the entire life of the school going on, and yet be removed sufficiently from it.

One day while John was sitting with him, Jason saw Mr Solomon climbing the steps of the hill with his exercise books under his arm.

'Who is that queer little clown?' he asked.

'Who?' John looked over the rail. 'Oh, that's Mr Solomon,' he answered.

'What does he come here for?'

'He teaches,' John said.

'Gosh!' Jason exploded.

'What's the matter?'

'I'm not going to have any old nigger teaching me!' Jason muttered.

Unnoticed by the boys Mrs Grant had come up behind Jason's chair.

'He's not "any old nigger", he's Mr Solomon,' she said in a voice which was not so much reproachful as sweetly reasonable. 'You remember the old woman in the hut where you left Pat?' she went on. 'He is her son.'

Jason remained silent. He remembered the books which were in the ramshackle house, and with anyone else he might have spoken of it. But Mrs Grant's 'reasonable' voice was quite unbearable, he decided.

'You see,' Mrs Grant went on. 'It's wartime, and so many of the regular members of the staff have joined up that it is very difficult to run the school at all.' Jason still remained obstinately silent. Without wanting to be, he was on bad terms with her again.

'I can't bear that Grant woman,' he said morosely to John afterwards.

'It's a pity,' John returned. 'Lots of the subjects you have are those she teaches. Science, you know, and geography, and all that. I find her all right.'

'You would,' Jason muttered. He was more depressed than usual after this, and welcomed the appearance of Goldbeard.

'When are you going to get off this verandah?' Dix asked.

'I get tired when I walk around,' Jason said. Goldbeard seemed to realize his mood, and while his blue eyes kept a sort of eagle look-out from the top verandah he encouraged Jason to talk to him.

'If I had only been sent to Canada!' Jason said regretfully. 'It's so far away from everything, out here.'

'Still, being on an island you may see more of the importance of a navy,' Dix suggested. 'Now, you hurry up and get well, and I'll have the small yacht brought around for you to play about with ... Ah, here is Mr Boomhill. Good afternoon, sir.'

It was uncanny the way Mr Boomhill always seemed to appear soon after Dix's arrival. His attitude was peculiar. Sometimes he seemed as if he were about to order Dix off the premises; and sometimes he seemed almost terrified of him. His mouth would fix itself in a disapproving way and his eyebrows would tilt up, and his scalp slide forward until Jason felt his fingers itch for a scalping knife. But to all these signs Dix appeared unconscious. He continued to speak in his bland, genial way to everyone, and to turn up at all sorts of odd hours, sometimes with Lady May, and sometimes without.

But if the Headmaster, and even Mr Jones disapproved of Goldbeard, it was nothing to the extraordinary fashion in which Andrew behaved in his presence. He had early taken advantage of having been in Jason's party from England, to display his intimacy by an early and unofficial visit to the sickroom where he had helped himself to the invalid's magazines and sweets until turned out by John at Jason's request. After this, in spite of rebuffs, he visited Jason regularly. Especially did he haunt the place whenever Lady May came.

'You haven't given me a commission yet,' he reminded her on her first visit to Jason when he waylaid her as she was going out. 'You said that you would let me run messages, with a bag, you know.'

'So I did,' exclaimed Lady May good-naturedly. 'Now, I tell you what. Here is a special commission. You know that the migratory birds from South America rest here on their way north and south? Well, they do. I want you to keep a sharp look-out for them. If you see them flying in flocks, or hear them flying at night, I want you to let me know. Sometimes they seem to be solitary, but they are usually in groups. I'll make you my chief bird-watcher on this coast.'

Andrew was slightly disappointed at this, as he had hoped for something more exciting. Besides, he rather thought that she was laughing at him. Still, he was a cheerful soul and made the best of it. Even in the presence of Lady May his behaviour towards Goldbeard was not entirely natural. Formerly he had attached himself firmly to his favourite, but now if he chanced to come in during one of Goldbeard's visits he would act in the most idiotic manner, pretend to shadow-box someone larger than himself, and would look so mysterious, so knowing that Jason longed to kick him.

One day John and Jason decided to corner him and make him confess what he was up to. When, therefore, Dix said 'good-bye' and left, and Andrew was slipping slyly in his wake, John got hold of him by the arm and dragged him to where Jason reclined in his long chair, and compelled him to kneel down on the floor between his two elders.

'Now,' said Jason, 'you'll kindly tell us what you mean by acting up as you do.'

'Let me go! I don't know what you mean, you bully!' Andrew began indignantly.

'And just keep your voice down. We don't want anyone overhearing this conversation, little one,' John said lazily.

'I'll shout,' Andrew said defiantly. 'Then you'll jolly well soon see that I'm not without friends!'

'All your sweet little playmates are in the singing class. They're cutting up such a shindy that they'd never hear you.'

On reflection Andrew decided that this was so. From the room on the other side of the schoolhouse there was such a bellow of 'John Peel' that any cries for help would have been drowned. Andrew, being a monotone of great power, had been forbidden to sing, much to his surprise.

'Well, what do you want with me?' Andrew demanded.

'Just tell us why you always sneak in here when Dix comes, and why you act like a mysterious sleuth all the time he's here.'

'Well, if you don't know, you're deaf and dumb and blind.'

'If we don't know what?'

'Ouch, let me go! You're crackers!'

'About what?'

'If you don't know how Goldbeard got hold of that paper.'

'What is he talking about?' Jason asked. John was silent. He had heard versions of it, but preferred not to think of it. 'Come, cough it out!' Jason demanded.

'Well, the day after we got here Goldbeard dropped a paper on the beach, and I used it to pack my treasures in, and brought them back to the College.'

'What treasures, you lunatic?'

'He went for an early morning sprint by himself on the beach,' John explained, 'and brought back a loathsome mess of shells and slugs and things.'

'They weren't loathsome. Wait until you see my collection! Mr Jones has helped me to put them in bottles and label them,' Andrew said defensively.

'Well, stick to the point. What about a paper?' Jason commanded.

'Well, I walked as far as Goldbeard's boathouse, and saw him coming in a speedboat, and he had this paper in his pocket. So when it dropped out I shouted to him to ask if I could have it, and I thought he shouted back that I could. So I picked it up to wrap up my things in. And when I got back to school old Boomer asked me where I had got it from, and I told him. And Dix was there. Wasn't old Boomer in a state!' Andrew said with a reminiscent chuckle which was gleeful and scared at the same time.

'But why should he have been in a state?' Jason wanted to know.

'Because, you silly old donkey, it was a Trinidad paper of the day before, and Old Boomer said that there hadn't been a ship or plane in or out of the island for at least three days except ours. And he asked him how he had got hold of it. And he wouldn't say. He just took it, and went.'

Andrew was enjoying himself immensely by this time. He could see that he had made a deep impression.

'After that,' he said, 'I heard them talking.'

'Heard who talking, eavesdropper?'

'Old Boomer and The Jones.'

'When your ear was glued to the keyhole, pretty one?'

'They were talking in the cabins after swimming. I hadn't been in very long, but I had cut my foot on a rock, so I came out. And the other chaps hadn't come in yet. And Old Boomer said that the paper worried him horribly, and he had a good mind to go and report to the Governor. He said that Lady May was blind.'

'What absolute nonsense!' Jason said.

'You silly fathead,' Andrew whispered. 'Don't you know ... Haven't you heard about strangers who have been seen around the coasts? And what about the submarine which got our boat? What do you suppose? One could get a paper from an enemy submarine if one had a speedboat. Gold-beard's a ...'

John's hand closed over Andrew's mouth.

'Shut up!' he said briefly. He kept his hand over the struggling Andrew's face while he looked questioningly at Jason.

'Of course it's all rot,' Jason declared. 'He's heard something wrong, or made it all up ... or something. Anyhow, we'll make him promise not to go blabbing such stuff to other people.'

Andrew got his mouth free by biting John's palm sharply.

'It's not all rot,' he said. 'Anyhow, we are going to find out.'

'Who do you mean by "we"?' Jason demanded.

'The Secret Four,' Andrew said. He had not meant to let this escape him, and for a moment he paused.

'Secret Four?' Jason asked.

'I can't tell you about them.'

'I can guess,' John remarked, rubbing his hand. 'There are three other little blighters who play with Andrew in the garden. They are always stuffing sweets and sniggering and making goofy signs, and all that rot. Secret Society!'

'Anyhow, if there's any deadly secret we'll find it out,' Andrew declared.

'Deadly nursery rhymes!' Jason said disgustedly. 'I don't care what you do in your Secret Society as long as you keep well away from me. But there's one thing you must not do, and that is, to make poisonous little nuisances of yourselves about Dix. You are not going to bother him with your stupid little friends. If you do . . .'

'Look here,' Andrew said in a changed voice. 'You say it's all rot about Goldbeard's being in league with the enemy. You say there's nothing in it that he had the paper. Well, here's something to think about. Where was he the morning we got in, before we were torpedoed? We couldn't find him on board, could we? And why couldn't we? Because he wasn't on board, see?'

'Where was he, then, you fathead?'

'I don't know. But he wasn't on board.'

'You're mad.'

'I'm not. You remember that we stayed outside the island all night? Well, next morning I searched all over the ship to find him, to ask about my notebook. And I couldn't find him. We wanted him to point out Badanda College to us, didn't we?'

'That doesn't prove anything. He might have been in the captain's cabin.'

'Well, listen. John went overboard after Guy, didn't he, when the ship was torpedoed? And when Jason was lugging Pat all over the place, what was happening to me? I slid down the hull and crawled along the breakwater, but the other way, out to sea. And there I saw Goldbeard coming towards the harbour in a boat with an outboard motor.'

'How could he? What do you mean?' Jason exclaimed.

'I don't know. But he must have known that the ship was going to be torpedoed, because he took jolly good care not to be on it at the time.'

'How could he have got off?' John asked.

'I don't know. But it was perfectly calm. He could have had a boat to meet him. There were plenty of fishing-boats sailing by.'

There was a long pause. Then Jason said in a savage voice:

'I don't believe one word of it.'

'Goldbeard took me into his boat. Didn't we come and pick you and Guy up, John?' Andrew demanded.

John said nothing.

'There you are!' Andrew said.

'I suppose you've gone and spun this yarn to all your Secret Brothers,' Jason said bitterly. Andrew looked at him. Then he looked at John.

'No,' he said in a frightened voice, quite unlike any that he had previously used. 'No ... I haven't told anyone but you two ... Not even Mrs Grant. I never really thought about it, or worked it out until ... Until I found out about the paper.'

'Well, get along now! I'm sick of you,' Jason said savagely. 'And keep your mouth shut, do you hear?' he added. Andrew got up. He hesitated as if he wished to appeal to them, but his two elders were staring out over the verandah rail with set faces. They did not seem to notice him when he departed.

CHAPTER 12

Jason Picks up the Threads

As he grew stronger Jason could not help feeling more cheerful. He took his place in the school, and in spite of the fact that some of his lessons were with Mrs Grant he found them quite bearable. He had been able to keep his vow about not learning Latin from Mr Solomon, for the reason that the old man had declined to teach him. Jason never knew whether he guessed the antagonism which he felt towards him, but at any rate Mr Solomon had said to Mr Boomhill:

'I cannot undertake to teach the two new older boys. As you know, I have no degree, and have not been used to teaching boys older than eleven. They do not fit into my classes, and I have all that I can handle at present.'

The result was that Mr Boomhill himself had to take them. He was doing a great deal of war work, and grumbled that he had no time to devote to such coaching. The result was scarcely happy, but Jason and John said nothing about it. Within a few weeks the island settled down into its former tranquil ways. Shops and houses in the burnt-out portion of the town were beginning to be rebuilt. The school jogged along in its routine, and the boys began to feel that they had been there always. The odd meal hours, the tropical food—flying-fish for breakfast at half-past ten in the morning, and the abundant and curious fruit – all these things lost their strangeness. Volunteer duty demanded less time from the staff. Fishermen set out in their fleets again. Everything was as normal as it could be under war conditions.

Jason found, as Goldbeard had thought he would, a very great delight in boating. Dix kept his promise to sail his little yacht around to the school lagoon, and with the help of the boatmen they managed to put it into order. Jason spent many hours of his convalescence learning to handle the yacht within the shelter of the reef. John was often his companion, but a good deal of his free afternoon time he spent in playing the organ in the church. One could reach it from the College either by going up to the main road, or by following a small track through the garden over the higher slopes of the hill. Usually John took the small path which came out on the main road just opposite the church. He often, in the beginning, asked Jason to go with him; but Jason was not fond of music, and gradually they grew accustomed to going their own ways.

The church was a picturesque little building made of stone. There were hanging oil lamps for evening services, but when John went to practise in the afternoons he sometimes had to light candles on either side of the organ loft, as the dusk fell suddenly and completely at about six o'clock. He did not often stay until six. The boys were not supposed to be out after sundown, as malarial mosquitoes might be found at that time in some seasons of the year. When the bell rang for Preparation they all trooped into the Hall to do their homework, and Jason and John would spend the evening hours together.

One day on leaving the church at the usual time John was surprised to see Goldbeard's car drawn up at the side of the road at the place where the little path sloped off down the hill. John hesitated, looking up and down the road, but the owner of the car was nowhere to be seen. It was quite clear and bright, as the full moon had risen, and the sunset was still red in the west. John stepped between the trees which stood on either side of the beginning of the path, and paused for a moment to enjoy the view. It was one of the loveliest evenings he could remember. The sea was all red and gold though the rim of the sun had just disappeared into the Caribbean. Light was still reflected down from the high clouds, and into the dazzle the Five Fishers stretched like a long thin finger, the top of each island hiding the strait between it and the next.

Someone was coming across from the First Fisher towards

College Beach. The tide was so low that a long-legged person could leap from rock to rock and come over dry-shod. The sunset glow shone full on the white-clad figure whom John recognized at once as Goldbeard. There was no mistaking that head and beard.

'He'll be coming up here to his car,' John said to himself. He resolved to wait for him. The first bell sounded. This was a warning to the boys to finish off whatever they were doing and to look for their books. It would not take John two minutes to get there, and he stood in the shadow of the trees waiting for Goldbeard to come up the hill. A few paces on from where he stood the track cut across the one which led towards the College, on the left. If one turned right, one could reach Dix's house a mile to the right. Straight ahead the track plunged steeply towards the beach. This path wound in its lowest part between scrubby bushes and rocks, and it was not until Goldbeard had cleared these that John saw that he was carrying something in his hand. It looked like a metal box with a long handle, and it seemed to be heavy.

Goldbeard climbed the path steadily until he reached the intersecting track, and then he hesitated. For a moment he seemed as though he were going to turn towards his own house. Then he glanced at the box, weighed it several times doubtfully, and seeming to make up his mind, he parted some bushes on the side of the path, and disappeared from view. John heard a great rustling as if he were digging in a pile of leaves. In a few moments he reappeared without his load, rubbing his hands, wiped them on his handkerchief, and walked briskly off in the direction of his own house. In a few seconds he had disappeared. He had not seen John, who, when he had gone, resumed his usual unhurried way towards the school. He could not tell why he had not called out to Goldbeard, except that he had seemed to be absorbed in what he was doing.

The sunset had faded from sea and sky. Now the Fishers lay, dark and mysterious, on the shining moonlit sea. It was a queer sort of night. When he had entered the College

John saw Goldbeard with a box in his hands

grounds he thought he saw shadows moving amongst the bushes, and now and then he thought he heard a footfall which was not an echo of his own. John was not a nervous person as a rule, but to-night he wondered if small wild animals were wandering in the woods. Mr Boomhill had said that there were no dangerous animals. He wondered what could be classified as dangerous. Perhaps, he thought, some of the captive creatures in the private zoo had escaped and were enjoying their freedom in the moonlight.

Just then something brushed his neck. He slapped at it. Again he felt it. He swung around and caught hold of the end of a long, thin switch which broke off in his hand. A few steps further on something struck him sharply on the knee. He grasped at a denser patch of shade and found that he had caught hold of a small boy.

'Pip! pip! pip!' squeaked the shadow. 'Rescue!'

'Rescue!' shouted three voices amongst which John thought he recognized Andrew's well-known squeak. Immediately he was charged by three seeming goats which butted him, prodded him, and tried to drag his captive from him. Putting his head down, John picked up his prisoner, and rushed him across the lawn to the verandah. The three rescuers clung valiantly to his legs.

'Let him go! Let him go!' Andrew panted.

'Let him go!' squealed Jack and Bruce.

'Take him. I don't want him!' John said, pitching Robin expertly into a prickly bush.

'Anyway, we tracked you all right,' Andrew said, as the two others rescued their leader from his painful predicament.

'We're Red Indians,' Andrew explained cheerfully. 'Tracking our enemies in the forests.'

'Aren't you supposed to be in Prep?' John asked.

'The second bell hasn't gone yet.'

'Let's have another round before we go in!' Jack suggested.

'I'll be Chief!' burst simultaneously from the throats of the Secret Four. The lively battle which ensued lasted until the second bell went, and all four boys went reluctantly in.

As John went to put away his music he caught sight of

Pat standing alone in a corner of the verandah, waiting for the boys of his age to come in with Mr Jones, who usually read to them for half an hour, as the little ones did not have homework to do. Andrew rushed past him with a casual, 'Hello, Pat!' It seemed scarcely possible that Pat had been one of their party all the way from England. Now they scarcely saw him.

'Pat seems rather out it, don't you think?' he said absently to Jason, who was waiting for him on the stairs.

'You needn't bother your head about him,' Jason said in a disgusted tone. 'Here, John,' he added, 'Old Boomerang has given us these cards to make out for him. We're to be excused Prep, and we're to go into the playroom to do them.'

'What are they?' John wanted to know.

'Some filthy things for to-morrow.'

'What's so special about to-morrow?'

'It's Founder's Day. Haven't you heard about it at Prayers every morning for the last week?'

'I'd forgotten all about it,' said John lazily. 'Sports and what not, I suppose. What do we have to do, particularly?'

'Divide the school into lots alphabetically, and enter them for team games and so on.'

'Do we have to go in for these bursts of fun?'

'I've volunteered to help, and put you down, too. So we don't have to run about with the infants.'

'Wise old egg!' John said. 'What are you doing here, Andrew?' he added as Andrew entered.

'I've finished my Prep, and The Jones says I can go on classifying my collection,' Andrew said.

'Well, get to the other end of the room. We don't want you here.'

'It's not your playroom,' Andrew said cheekily.

While he was dragging his bundle out of his locker John went back to his first idea.

'All the same,' he said, 'it seems to me that Pat ought to go around with the others more. He never seems to do anything with the boys.'

'I think he gets too much attention,' Jason said. 'He's always having tea on the Grants' verandah instead of in the schoolroom. Dix is always there playing with those kids, and Lady May comes over and takes him back with her to Government House. I can't think why they all waste their time over him. Except for his beastly puzzles and machines he's a stupid kid.'

'You're jealous!' Andrew hissed, about an inch from Jason's ear.

'Hop it, you scavenger!' John said, as Jason flushed.

'Go and label yourself as a sea-slug!' Jason growled.

'My collections are valuable,' Andrew said with dignity. 'I'm making a marine museum, and someday it will be in a large marble building and everyone will read my name over the door. I'll be as famous as Pat's father.'

'Don't waste time about it,' Jason advised, taking out his handkerchief and preparing to flick Andrew's knees. Andrew sheered off and went back to his work.

'Perhaps it's because his father is so famous that they make much of him,' John suggested in a low tone.

'Doesn't make sense to me,' Jason said. 'In any case, why should Dix waste his time talking to him? He'll never be keen on boxing, or any other kind of sport.'

John opened his mouth to say that he had seen Dix that evening, but he changed his mind. Instead, he asked:

'Is there anything besides swimming for to-morrow's competition?'

'Yes. Here's the list: rowing, diving, sand-castles – that's for the infants – fishing, gymnastics, and a Surprise Event after tea.'

'What sort of Event?'

'I haven't the vaguest. All I know is that Boomerang and The Jones have been whispering and chuckling about it, and measuring off the ground, and rushing in and out of the grounds, and looking over their shoulders ... Crazy as loons, both of them. That's going to wind up the day, and Lady May is going to give out the prizes.'

'With special award to Mr Andrew Thomson,' said a smug voice behind them, 'for gaining most points in all the events, and in the Intelligence Tests.'

'Since you are so intelligent,' John said, 'you may make out these lists for us. Here we are. We've divided the names. All you have to do is to copy them on to the lists.'

'Right oh!' Andrew said with alacrity. He loved lists. But a stronger inducement still was the idea that he could manage to put all of the Secret Four into one team instead of dividing them alphabetically and allowing them to be mixed with other lots. Andrew grinned as he worked, elated at his own cleverness. He did not realize that by doing this he was going to expose the Secret Four to the ridicule of the school.

CHAPTER 13

A Secret Event with a Surprising Outcome

ANDREW was the first to awake on Founder's Day. He had intended to stay awake all night, but somehow his eyes had closed as soon as he got into bed, and the night passed in a flash. However, he had the consolation of knowing that he had opened his eyes before anyone else. He stole across the dormitory and pulled Robin by the toe: a secret sign, and the other two were awakened similarly. The idea had been that on this important day they could do all sorts of things before the rest of the world woke up. They intended to sleuth around and find out what the Surprise Event was to be. But somehow, once they were dressed, they could not think how to set about it.

'Let's put a message under The Jones's door,' Andrew suggested.

'What about?'

'Well, to warn him that he's being sleuthed. Let's find something to write on. Look, these big leaves will do.'

A sheaf of leaves gathered, Andrew had another brilliant idea.

'Let's send him a lot of messages, all day long.'

'But about what, man?'

'Oh, all kinds of things. And let's write them all backwards.'

'Why not in our own code?'

'It takes too long,' Andrew said truthfully. 'And I can't always decipher them myself. But I can write quite fast backwards. I've been practising ... About as fast as I can frontwards.'

A short time after this Mr Jones woke up from a dream of being stung on his nose by a wasp, and found that something which he had blown into the air by a violent sneeze was fluttering down on his face. He sat up at once and looked around. Insects interested him, but not in bed. He was relieved to see that what had tickled him was only a leaf. It did not at first occur to him that a leaf should not have been there, nor that the scrawls on the leaf were words. However, when, after he had got up, he found another leaf on his dressing-table, and another in his shaving-mug, he

Mr Jones found another leaf when he was shaving

recollected that it was Founder's Day. He looked at the leaves more carefully, and it finally occurred to him that they had been written on. Long experience with boys made him hold the leaves against a mirror one by one, and there he read, 'A surprise is in store'; 'To-day is the day it will be revealed'; and 'Look out for strange things'.

Mr Jones would have been very busy all that day in any case, but Andrew found the means to make him busier still.

At short intervals all the morning messages delivered by
unseen hands warned him that *An Unknown danger has to be
faced*, *The Secret is not what you think;* and that the *End of the
Day will bring an end worse than the Beginning.*

'Nice lads,' chuckled Mr Jones. 'They take such an
interest!' None of their efforts, however, revealed to the
Secret Four what the Surprise Event was to be.

Morning School was half an hour shorter than usual.
Then the boys were separated into teams, and the prelimin-
ary heats were run. Points scored by the winners in all the
events counted towards the credit of the teams. Somehow
it never occurred to anyone that the Secret Four should not
have all been in one team, and they enjoyed themselves
hugely. Andrew was particularly pleased with himself for
having arranged this. In the swimming events Andrew was
naturally something of a handicap, but he managed to hook
a small fish and a crab in the fishing tries. It was sheer luck,
but gained him points. Climbing ropes had earned him the
nickname of Monkey, and gained some more points for his
team. Altogether, the Secret Four were quite proud of
themselves by tea-time.

Lady May and other distinguished guests now arrived,
and Jason was most interested in a contingent of Naval
Officers who had come to the island for a holiday. One of
them, to whom Mr Boomhill was particularly hearty, was
an old boy of the school, and this reconciled Jason somewhat
to his lot. Tea, which was served in the pavilion, was truly
magnificent. There were four kinds of ice-cream served in
cones: chocolate, mango, coconut, and vanilla. Old Dinah had
sent down a collection of cakes which took even Andrew's
breath away, and kept him speechless for some time.

After tea Mr Boomhill stood up, and in an expectant
silence, made his speech. Every year on Founder's Day, he
said, the school enjoyed some sort of Surprise. Once it had
been a play by the staff. Another year it had been theatricals
by a visiting company on its way to South America. Once
they had had a concert. This time he had arranged something entirely new. His face was wreathed in smiles. 'Will

the captain of each team step forward,' he concluded, 'and receive from Mr Jones the instructions about this Surprise Event?' The boys came forward and were handed envelopes. 'In each envelope,' Mr Boomhill explained, 'are consecutively numbered slips. Each is a little verse which is a clue, and each must be solved in its turn in order that the one that follows may be understood. The last clue leads to hidden treasure. We have taken pains to ensure that, though all the teams must finally arrive at the same place, they will follow different routes, covering about equal distances. When the treasure is found, the winning team is to bring it back here, first giving a whistle to notify the others that the hunt is over.'

'A Treasure Hunt! How exciting!' Lady May exclaimed. 'Why don't you allow us all to take part, Mr Boomhill? I've always wanted to dig for buried treasure. This is the very place! Here on the shores of the Spanish Main there must be loads of it!'

The Headmaster beamed. 'Too late to join in this time, Lady May,' he said. 'The teams have already started. And, if I am not mistaken, they will be fully occupied for the next hour.'

'What do we do now?' John asked in an undertone, as he and Jason stood above, a little apart from the circle of distinguished guests.

'Hang around and wait, I suppose,' Jason answered. 'I wish we could go for a swim. I'm boiling hot. But I suppose it wouldn't do.'

A strange young man came running down the steps from the College, and Jason asked:

'Who's that? Another distinguished guest?'

'He's an A.D.C. at Government House,' John answered. 'We saw him when we first arrived. His name's Allen. He's something to do with the Police. He's been around at the College with Lady May a couple of times. Decent chap.'

'Hello, John,' Allen said, coming up to them. 'How are things going? Are the Important Persons all occupied? I need a cooler. How far have you got in the programme of events?'

'They're having a Treasure Hunt,' said John.

'Good. That'll keep them busy for a time. I'll go and have a word with Mr Boomhill and Lady May, and see if they'll excuse me while I have a swim. I'm supposed to be driving Lady May home. I say, why don't you both come in with me?'

'I'd like to,' John said, and Jason looked eager.

Allen went up to the pavilion, spoke to Lady May and Mr Boomhill, and to a few others, and came back in a few minutes with Goldbeard, who, it seemed, also had a swimming suit with him. Mr Boomhill had kindly consented to the two boys going for a swim while they were waiting for the teams to finish, and it was with considerable pleasure that they went to change. The day had been definitely boring up till now.

'We'll make the best of it,' Goldbeard said as they ran down to the beach. 'We may have only a few minutes. It wouldn't do not to be there when the great Surprise Event finished.'

It was the best swim the boys had had for a long time. Twenty minutes later they were still out on the raft, murmuring idly that they really ought to go in. Since the Treasure Hunt had started, the teams had been out of sight, and comparatively quiet. Now suddenly there was a hubbub of voices, not from one, but from three places at once, where it sounded as if small boys were crashing through bushes and long grass, and screaming with the excitement of discovery. Then three whistles sounded.

Dix was staring up the hill. Some of the voices and whistles came from quite far away towards the end of the school property, below where the roof of the little church showed through the trees on the summit.

'We'd better get back,' he said in a curious tone, and dived off without stopping to explain. He swam powerfully back to the shore, and as the others followed him towards the dressing cabins, saw Mr Boomhill standing on the steps of the pavilion talking to Mr Jones.

'There must be some mistake,' Mr Boomhill was booming forth. 'There's only *one* treasure, but three parties seem to think they have found it.'

'What fun!' Lady May exclaimed. 'I wonder what the other two have unearthed?'

'I can't think!' he returned. As always, when things went wrong, his eyebrows went up and his scalp slid forward.

'We've found it! We've found it!' three separate chants of victory rose through the trees.

'I love this!' Lady May laughed. 'I think it's the jolliest thing I ever heard of! Three Treasures! Didn't I tell you that there must be loads of buried treasure?'

'But it's all wrong,' Mr Boomhill said crossly. 'They could not have read the clues properly.'

'Never mind! Let them all bring their treasures,' Lady May said. 'It will be such fun to see what they have found!'

'Very well,' said the Headmaster, making an effort to get his eye-brows and scalp in their proper places.

When Dix and Allen and the two boys came back from their bathe, three victorious teams were standing before the steps of the pavilion. The table full of prizes had been pulled in front of the semi-circle of chairs where the Distinguished Guests sat. Allen and Dix went up and stood behind them.

'We're ready,' called Mr Boomhill. 'Let the first team come forward, and show their treasure.'

'They've found a box, but it may be an empty one,' called Mr Jones.

'It's not empty! It's heavy, and it rattles!' cried the team.

'Then let it be brought forward,' Mr Boomhill shouted gaily. He seemed to wish to imitate Lady May's high spirits.

The leaders of the team advanced carrying a tin box between them. The Secret Four, who were among the unsuccessful teams had pressed to the front rank of spectators. Suddenly they clutched each other in dreadful foreboding. It was their Secret Box. In silent agony they saw the lid prised open. The tin, held upside down by Mr Jones, let out a stream of lollipops, a pile of forbidden comics, four red mugs, and the notebook which held all their secrets, codes and all!

Lady May's laughter could be heard above the general merriment. Even Mr Boomhill's 'Ho! Ho!' was hearty.

'Well, though this is not the treasure, I think you should have a consolation prize for having discovered it,' he declared. 'So we will award these ... er ... lollipops to this team. You all know, of course, that all sweets must be kept in the tuck cupboard under the care of Miss Hall. Mr Jones will please dispose of the comics as they also are contraband. As for the mugs ...' He picked them up, and then the notebook. The Secret Four sought desperately to creep backwards through the crowd, but found their way firmly blocked by boys determined to miss none of the fun. 'If the names in this book are anything to go by,' the Headmaster continued, in a bantering tone, 'we may take it that these four mugs belong appropriately to Robin, Jack, Bruce, and Andrew. Will they please claim their property?' Willing hands pushed the Secret Four to the foot of the steps. To tremendous applause and laughter they were forced to take a mug each before they could escape.

'It was the clue that made us think we were right, sir,' the disappointed leader of the team said.

'What was it? Read it,' Mr Boomhill was beginning to show some irritation again.

'This sir,

"Bush above the ancient stone,
    Where the treasure lies alone".'

'It was under a stone, with a dead bush on top,' the team added.

'But didn't your final clue tell you that the Treasure was not concealed from sight?' Mr Boomhill asked. He raised his voice and rolled off the couplet:

' "Lies the Treasure, full in sight,
    Lit with sunset's rosy light." '

'Dear me, Mr Boomhill, you are a poet!' Lady May exclaimed as the team retired crestfallen.

The second team, confident of success, came forward next, with a 'treasure' that seemed very heavy. As soon as John set eyes on it, he looked across at Dix. This was the box which Goldbeard had carried up the steep path the day before. Jean and Pat had squeezed in front of this man of mystery, and he was staring over their heads. John could not help thinking what a protection a beard was. It completely masked Dix's expression. There was a silence while the Headmaster looked at the object which had been placed before him.

'Well,' he said at last in a puzzled tone. 'This is certainly not the Treasure you were meant to discover. What it is, I really cannot say. Can you open it, Mr Jones?' Jones went down on one knee. John gave another furtive glance up at Goldbeard who sat absolutely motionless. Pat had taken a step forward, and now stood with his hand on the post of the balustrade of the steps, looking down at the strange metal box with which the master was fiddling.

'Here's a catch,' Mr Jones said. 'Ah ... It opens ...' Everyone pressed forward to see what was inside. 'I can't make out what it is,' he said at last.

'It's a transmitter,' a small voice announced gravely, in the puzzled silence.

The Naval Officer suddenly stood up. 'Let me have a look at that,' he said. He ran down the steps and stooped beside Mr Jones.

'Yes, by Jove, it is a transmitter,' he said. 'And, I rather think, one of a new type used by the enemy. But there is something missing. Did you boys open it when you found it?'

'No, sir,' a chorus of voices replied.

'Where was it?'

'Near the top of the hill, sir.'

'In the College grounds?' Mr Boomhill asked.

'No, sir ...'

'What made you go searching outside the boundaries?' Mr Boomhill asked sharply. 'Didn't the clues say to stay within them?'

'Well, it wasn't far outside, and we got a bit confused, sir, and then when we found this we thought we must have got it right after all.'

'Where exactly was it?'

'Underneath a pile of leaves . . .' Trouble seemed to be brewing, and the Head snapped back:

'The clues said quite clearly that the Treasure was open to the air. I should never bury treasure under anything of that sort, because of snakes and insects, and so on. We would not expose them to any risk,' he added, glancing back at Lady May as if clearing himself.

'If you do not mind, sir,' Allen said suddenly, 'I will take charge of this treasure trove. It is most likely the property of some government department, and should be returned to it.'

'But I assure you,' the officer said with considerable excitement, 'that this is most important. We must find out all about it at once.'

'I assure you that everything necessary will be done,' Allen said. He picked up the box and turned away. 'I presume I may take this into safe keeping?' he asked Lady May, 'I will be back for you very shortly.'

'Certainly, certainly,' she said, looking with unrestrained curiosity at the box.

Mr Boomhill looked in an irritated way at Allen. He did not like anything to upset his arrangements, and the glorious Treasure Hunt was beginning to wear an air he did not at all like.

'Now, boys,' he said, 'be so good as to read out the clue which led you to believe that this must be the treasure.'

The leader produced a crumpled slip of paper and started to read in a low tone.

'Speak up, man!' barked the Head.

' "Underneath the leafy shade
    Is the costly treasure laid," ' the boy repeated woodenly.

'That's why we looked under the leaves, sir,' said another of the team.

'Leafy *shade!*' the Head repeated. 'Shade, not blanket. And you forgot the first instruction,

    "Between it and your eyes no screen,
       So it shall be freely seen." '

The sound of his verse pleased Mr Boomhill, and he repeated it three or four times in a booming voice.

'You should have known from that that the Treasure was not where you looked for it.'

'Yes, sir,' said the disappointed leader.

'Well, well,' Mr Boomhill mopped his neck and forehead with a large white handkerchief. 'It's getting late. But there is still the real Treasure—and here it comes at last.' He led the clapping which the boys kept up so long and with such enthusiasm that he had difficulty in getting silence again.

The winning team stood beside their find, a small tin chest, and, on being told to open it, displayed a badminton set.

'All right, and very nice,' John murmured in Jason's ear, 'but more like a gift to the school than to the team. I suppose we'll all be allowed to play with it?'

'Now for the prizes,' said Mr Boomhill, turning to the table. There was a little stir and bustle among the boys as Mr Jones marshalled the winners into line to come up as their names were called. John, who had taken no part, gave way, until he found himself at the back of the crowd. The Naval Officer who had shown such interest in the Transmitter had not gone back to his place amongst distinguished guests. He had been talking to the members of the team who had found it.

'I should like to go and examine the place at once,' he said to Mr Jones. 'Allen's all right, but I feel that a person who has special knowledge of these things should take charge.'

'It's very strange,' murmured Mr Jones, 'but I have been receiving warning messages all day.' His eyes were almost popping out of their glasses, and his Adam's apple worked up and down.

'What kind of messages?'

'Telling me that something unusual and strange was to happen before the end of the day. I thought at first it was a joke of the boys. But now I am beginning to think that they might be connected with this extraordinary discovery.'

'I should strongly advise you to put all such messages in the hands of the police,' said the Naval Officer.

'I will do so at once,' Mr Jones agreed rather flustered, 'at least, as soon as the prize-giving is over.'

John felt a tug at his coat : turning, he saw Andrew.

'John!' Andrew said. 'I want to talk to you. I must.'

'What's all the hurry?' John said. 'They're going to give the prizes now.'

'I must talk to you. Do come!' Andrew said tensely. His eyes were so horrified behind his glasses, and his ears stood out in so distracted a fashion that John felt compelled to follow him.

'Well, what is it?' he asked, allowing himself to be led away among the trees. 'No one can hear you,' he said. 'Get on with it. They are making such a row with clapping that you could talk out loud and no one would hear you. Hurry up.'

Andrew gulped several times.

'It's about that second Treasure,' he said at last. 'You know very well who put it there in the pile of leaves. I saw you, and I saw him. I was in our secret hiding place, and saw you both. You know it was Goldbeard.'

'Do the other boys know?' John asked.

'No. They had gone into ambush farther along, waiting for you to come down. I gave the signal when you started on again.'

'Well, hold your tongue,' said John.

'But I must go to tell Mr Jones about the messages, and he may ask me ... I'm so afraid I may tell.'

'What messages?' John asked.

'You heard what The Jones said about the messages he had been receiving all day. I sent them.'

'Why?'

'Just for fun,' said Andrew miserably. 'We thought it would be a joke to get old Jones all hot and bothered, thinking that we had guessed the Surprise Event. So we kept sending him messages all day. I wrote them backwards on leaves,' he babbled.

'You are the world's champion meddler,' John said at last.

'But you see, I've got to tell him about them, or he'll go to the police,' Andrew almost wept.

'Well, go, then,' said John. 'Go before he has time do anything. He won't beat you. They don't in this school. Was it you who wrote the messages, or all of you?'

'I thought of them and wrote them,' Andrew said, with a touch of pride. 'And I thought of writing them backwards on leaves.'

'You would!' John said. 'But I think,' he added, 'that it would be best for you to take your three pretty friends with you when you confess. Because you are not to say one word, mind you, about Goldbeard. And since the others don't know, they won't force you to tell. Now, remember, not one word!'

'I'll do my best,' said Andrew, taking a long, brave breath.

'You jolly well will,' said John, taking hold of his arm. 'And to make sure of it, I'm going to go and stand behind you while you're speaking to The Jones. So come along.'

CHAPTER 14

Jason Wishes He Had Gone to the Picnic

THE day after Founder's Day was Wednesday, a half-day. Dix had arranged to give the yacht a trial with the boys. When Jason was ready to go down to the beach, however, he could not find John anywhere.

'He must have gone already,' he thought crossly, but when he arrived at the boathouse Dix was in the yacht alone.

'Where's John?' Jason and Dix said at the same instant.

'I thought he would be here,' Jason said. 'Do you think he's swimming?' He looked towards the raft, but could not see him amongst the crowd.

'He'll soon be down,' Dix said. 'Let's go ahead. After all, we're not going out of the lagoon. When we see him we'll come back.'

But John did not come down to the beach all the afternoon, and when Dix said good-bye at sunset they had not seen a sign of him.

As Jason was going across the verandah however, he met John coming along with his music under his arm.

'Where've you been?' he cried.

'To practise.'

'And forgot about the yacht?'

John hesitated.

'We waited for you quite a time.' John was still silent. 'What's the matter?' Jason asked.

'Nothing,' John said. 'But I'm late. Must put away my music.'

Jason stared after him. He waited until John got his books and they went together into Hall.

'I can't think what's the matter with you,' Jason whispered, when they were sitting in their places. John pretended not to hear him. Jason worked for a time. Then he wrote a note and put it on John's desk. John picked it up and read

it, screwed it up into a ball and forced it into his inkwell.
'You don't believe that rot that Andrew said about Dix, do
you?' Jason had written. John, with his chin on his hands,
seemed engrossed in his work. Nothing he could say would
help. He had seen Dix carrying the metal box, and knew
that he had buried it where it had been found. He longed
to talk it out with Jason, but he couldn't . . . not yet.

After that evening Jason would not speak to John except
when he had to. They continued to sit together at table and
in Hall; but apart from a mere 'Pass the bread', 'the salt,
please', or 'a letter for you,' they did not speak. None of
the old banter and fun enlivened their days.

This state of affairs was made worse by the wild rumours
which went flying from mouth to mouth. The box had
definitely contained a wireless transmitter. It was certain
proof that enemy agents had been on the island. Excitement
ran nearly as high as it had when the submarine had
attacked the harbour. In the weeks that followed the cold-
ness between Jason and John settled into a permanent state.
A few times Jason tried to have it out in words: but John,
usually so easy going, now seemed wrapped in reserve.

'What's happened to John?' Dix asked, once or twice.

'Swatting or practising,' Jason had answered. Dix had
asked no more questions. He seemed as genial as ever, gave
the boys rides in his speedboats, and came and went without seeming to notice if anyone looked at him mistrustfully.

So time went on until it approached the day on which the
College had its annual picnic at Coconut Reach. This was
a stretch of sand on the other side of the island which was
bordered by plantations of coconut palms. At one end was
a lighthouse on a rocky promontory, and nearby was a
village where donkeys could be hired. The scenery was quite
different from that of College Beach, and the boys felt, after
a day at Coconut Reach, that they had been away for a
change. They usually went in special buses which took the
main road across the north end of the island. They spent
the day visiting the lighthouse, fishing, swimming, or riding
donkeys, and had a camp fire at the beach.

'I would like you two boys to go in the first bus,' Mr Jones said to Jason and John the day before the picnic. He was arranging details of the picnic, and did not seem to notice that the boys were not on speaking terms.

'If you don't mind, sir,' Jason said, 'I would rather not go.'

'Why not?'

'It gives me a headache to be out in the sun all day.'

'You'll have to get permission from Mr Boomhill to stay at home,' Mr Jones said.

Mr Boomhill raised his eyebrows when Jason asked to be allowed to stay at the College next day.

'You are perfectly strong now, my boy,' he said.

'There's an awful glare from the sea at Coconut Reach in the morning, sir,' Jason said. 'And I don't feel very well.'

'There is plenty of shade under the coconuts,' the Headmaster said.

'Please, sir, I would rather not.'

'I will not force you to go, Jason,' Mr Boomhill said in displeasure. Jason averted his eyes so as not to see the mop of curly white hair sliding forward to join the uplifted eyebrows. 'Still,' he went on, 'this may be as good an opportunity as any for me to comment on your general conduct here. It has been apparent to me that you do not care to exert yourself to promote school activities. You have been ill, I know, and I have made allowances for you on that account. I will excuse you this time, but if you feel to-morrow morning that you can take your place with us, I shall be better pleased.'

In spite of this appeal to his conscience Jason did not join the party next morning. In fact, he took care to stay in the schoolroom while the boys were gathering round the buses. When they had all departed in high glee Jason heard Mr Boomhill say:

'I am going to be at Government House for lunch, Miss Hall.' Soon after this he left in his car.

'You'll be rather lonely, I'm afraid, Jason,' Miss Hall said, looking into the schoolroom.

'I'll be all right,' Jason said. 'I think I'll go for a walk.'

'Better not go too far, in case the sun gives you a head-ache,' she suggested slyly. 'The servants expect a sort of holiday,' she added, 'so you will have to put up with a cold snack at lunch.'

'Let me have some sandwiches,' Jason said. 'I'll eat them on the beach.'

'That's a good idea,' Miss Hall said.

Jason had not been farther than the grounds by himself before. He had been ill for nearly a month, and after that had not felt much like walking, so he really knew very little about the island. While he was waiting for the sandwiches, he went to the schoolroom to look at the folding map of Tripadoes which was spread on a side table. Badanda College was marked about three-quarters up the western coast. The main road of the island followed the coast for a couple of miles north of the College, and then cut across the island to the east coast over a central hump of hills. There was no road right around the island. Jason made up his mind to walk steadily until he reached the northern tip of the island, and then to make his way across country to a secondary road by which he might return. According to the map there were a couple of footpaths leading from the northern beach, and the hilly nature of the country prom-ised interesting walking. On impulse Jason folded up the map and pushed it into his pocket. Then when Miss Hall came back with the sandwiches he set off in the same direction which Andrew had taken on his first exploratory expedition.

It was a sparkling day, and his spirits rose after he had walked a mile or so along the beach. He wished that John were with him, and that they were not involved in this stupid misunderstanding. He resolved to make it up with him as soon as the day was over. The beaches were new to him and, like Andrew, he was curious to see what was beyond each headland. At every point he took out his map and identified it. There were no houses to be seen until he came to Dix's boathouse. Here, as Andrew had done, he paused to take breath at the top of the hillock which divided

Goldbeard's little inlet from the other beach, and, like Andrew, he did not at first see the boathouse which was built into the foot of the cliff. It was the sound of voices which attracted his attention, and peering over he saw two men standing knee-deep in water examining a boat which was half-awash. It looked as though it had been holed by a sharp point of rock, and there seemed very little water in the inlet. Jason remembered that Dix had said that he could only enter his own anchorage at high tide, and that was why he so often left his boat at the College pier. These two men were evidently in the midst of a heated argument, and though they kept their voices low the language which they spoke did not sound like English. As Jason watched, they seemed to take a decision, for they turned, and still wading knee-deep, began to bring the boat in to the boathouse. Jason waited until they were both fairly under its shelter, and then, slipping quietly down the steep track behind the cliff, he went on his way northwards. Looking back at the next point, he saw the familiar figure of Dix coming rapidly down the slope from the direction of his house, which Jason knew lay somewhere amongst the trees at the top of the ridge. Who were these men? Jason wondered. One was about his own height, a fair young fellow; and the other a stocky, bald-headed, sunburnt person of middle age. Whoever they were, they had evidently got caught in the receding tide, and had smashed their boat.

Jason kept steadily on until he judged it to be after midday. Then he sat down to eat his sandwiches on a shingly stretch covered with boulders which seemed to form the northern tip of the island. Lying in the shade of a rock which overhung another so as to form a rough cave, he fell asleep. When he awoke the shadows had moved so far that he thought it must be well into the afternoon. He resolved to leave the beach and to find his way through the wooded hills to the road. Before doing this he climbed to the top of a pinnacle of rock, and sat down on its summit to study the map. He could see through gaps in the trees what appeared to be a long wall. This, he decided, must be the wall of the

Isolation Hospital. According to the map the grounds were extensive, and the secondary road which he wished to reach was the boundary on the far side. By cutting through the woods he should get there without trouble.

As he sat there he felt that someone was staring at him, and turned to see a small negro boy looking over a sand-dune at him. There was fear in the child's popping eyes, but Jason did not give him another thought. He folded the map, put it away in his pocket, and started up the rough slope. He had grown rapidly since leaving England, and because of his illness had not become as tanned as the other boys. Even Pat was now quite sunburnt. But Jason was unusually fair, one of those who peel but don't easily darken with exposure to the sun. In his khaki shorts and shirt he seemed older than a boy of fourteen.

The little negro had disappeared, but in a few minutes Jason saw him again, and recognized him by a blue patch on the old yellow shirt which he wore. Now there were three little boys, and as he glanced up all three started to run. Jason paused to consult his map. The high wall of the hospital stretched to the left and ahead of him, with no gate in it on the seaward side. There seemed to be a collection of small huts to his right, and to avoid them he began to cut across some rough country, trying to make for the secondary road beyond. Suddenly a small crowd of people appeared directly in his path, as if waiting for him. Farther on someone was riding hastily along on a donkey. Jason continued on his way. The group of negroes waited silent until he came up, and then fell in behind him, pressing quite close to him. Jason stopped and looked round. The negroes stopped too, looking at him with fear, and something like hostility.

'Good afternoon,' Jason said, feeling that he must speak. What could they want? Did they mean to threaten him? Surely not. Boomhill and Mr Jones had repeatedly said how friendly the natives were.

'Good day,' they replied in chorus. Nothing more. Jason pretended to be interested in his map. They came up close and peered over his shoulder. Ahead, there was another group of people waiting. Wherever he looked, Jason suddenly saw knots of black people coming from nowhere, in a part of the island where one might have said that no one lived. By this time he was walking at the head of a sort of procession. He turned sharply once or twice, to shake them off, but wherever he went, they followed in purposeful silence. At last, in a group ahead, he saw a tall, powerfully built negro in a sort of uniform, who seemed to be able to command the others. He stopped directly in Jason's way.

'Good day,' he said, as the others had done.

'Good day,' Jason replied.

'Where you goin', sah?'

'I am going for a walk,' Jason answered, surprised.

'Where to, sah?'

'Nowhere in particular,' Jason answered. 'I'm just walking for exercise.'

'Why you don't walk along the road?'

'Why should I? I've just come off the beach.'

This created such a sensation that Jason looked around him in the greatest perplexity.

'I see him on de beach wid a map, Ramon,' piped up the first little negro.

Jason began to think that perhaps he had strayed into forbidden territory. This might be some military area, although there were no signs warning people off. It did not occur to him that his fairness, and his accent which was strange to them, not having the West Indian twang, might be counted against him. They also pointed to his map and looked at each other significantly.

Tired of being surrounded like this Jason faced about, meaning to retrace his steps to the beach, but made the mistake of walking hurriedly. The patter of bare feet along the path behind him soon warned him that he was being followed. He walked still faster. A shrill whistling sounded. He lost his head, and started to run. There was a shout: 'He runnin'! He runnin'!' and a stone whizzed past his ear, followed by a shower of them. One struck him on the

Jason stopped and looked round, and the negroes stopped too

F

shoulder. He burst desperately from the path in an effort
to shake them off among the trees, but in vain. He had
reached the very end of the island, and there was only one
way by which he could get back. Shorewards the grey wall
stretched without a break. It was not very high, and Jason,
running doggedly, decided to try to get over it and so to
shelter in the hospital. As he ran for it a shout told him that
he had been seen. He sprang, clutched the top of the wall,
and tried to drag himself up. A dozen hands grasped his legs.

'We got him!' 'Hold he, man!' 'Hol' 'at!'

'All right,' Jason yelled. 'Let go of me!' He loosened his
grip of the wall and fell back. In an instant they were on
top of him.

The large man, who had stood in his way, arrived.

'We got he, Ramon!' the others yelled.

'Get off me!' Jason panted. 'I won't run away.'

'No you won't, big boy!' someone remarked, and the
crowd laughed mockingly.

'Let he go,' the large man called Ramon. Jason got
slowly to his feet. He felt bruised and winded.

'What's the matter with all of you?' he said, trying to
keep his voice from shooting up into the treble squeak
which he hated. 'What do you think I am? Can't a person
walk in this part of the island? Let me go back to Badanda
College.'

'The College?' Ramon repeated, and the word was
echoed again and again by others in the group.

'Yes. I am at Badanda College.'

'Then why you ain't at de picnic at Coconut Reach?'
someone shouted.

'I didn't want to go,' Jason said, looking at the black,
suspicious faces round him. 'I came for a walk instead.'

'A walk wid a map!' shouted one of the boys, and the
others muttered darkly.

'Rope he up!' someone cried.

'Why are you behaving like this?' Jason asked. 'Who do
you think I am?' There was no answer, only a steady,
watchful look in all those eyes which frightened him. He

swallowed. 'Come,' he said to the big man in uniform who seemed more intelligent than the others, 'Is there a telephone anywhere about? Let me call the police.' He said this because he remembered suddenly that there was no one but Miss Hall at the school, and he did not wish to alarm her.

'He want de police?' Jason heard them murmur unbelievingly.

'They a telephone in de hospital,' Ramon said. 'Come.'

The crowd moved forward, with Jason in the middle, walking beside the big man. Ahead of him the smallest of the negro boys ran along backwards, to keep their eyes on Jason. Behind and on both sides the crowd pushed and jostled and whistled and muttered. Almost exhausted, his clothes torn and dusty, his face and hands and knees caked with dirt, Jason tried to muster a little dignity. They came to the road round the corner of the wall, then a few yards farther on, on the opposite side, a gravel path between hedges, evidently the private drive to a large house. If only someone would come along, someone who could extract him from this awful situation! Close on the wish came the sound of a car approaching, and the whole party hastily scattered towards the sides of the road. Dix was at the wheel. Behind him were the two men whom Jason had seen with the broken boat. His heart leapt, and he waved and shouted – but Goldbeard drove right past him, without even the flicker of an eyelash.

The negroes were quick to take advantage of his discomfort, and surrounded him again.

'Mr Dix you friend, white man?' one jeered. There were hoots of derisive laughter. Jason set his teeth and walked on. Then someone shouted, 'See ... Dere Sambo! Come, Sambo! We found de man.'

A tall, shambling black man with a rather foolish face came from a hut.

'Sambo! Sambo!' the crowd shouted.

'De man on de beach! De man on de beach! We got de man!'

The throng halted while Sambo was pushed forward to confront Jason.

'Is dis de man you see on de beach?' Ramon asked. 'De man wid de gun?'

'Yaas, dat de same man!' Sambo declared, staring at Jason, and looking up and down from his fair hair to his dusty gym shoes.

The crowd pressed closer, and there was an ominous murmuring.

'Come along,' the large man Ramon said. 'Come. We goin' to de hospital to telephone.'

Jason realized that they took him for a spy. He tried to think how to reason with them, but he realized that his safety lay with Ramon. As long as the crowd obeyed the large man he would at least be unhurt until the police arrived. He saw now that the uniform which Ramon wore was that of the hospital. A few yards farther on they arrived at the gates. The porter's lodge was just inside.

'Where is the telephone?' Jason demanded.

'Not here,' Ramon answered. 'They's one at de hospital. I sendin' someone to telephone. You go inside and wait.'

Jason went into the lodge, and sank into a chair as far from the window as he could get. The crowd muttered and whistled outside, and sometimes peeped through the door or the windows to goggle at him. He heard the large man instructing someone to go up to the hospital to telephone. He sat there sweating. His legs were trembling with fatigue, and his ears sang. After an endless seeming pause he heard a cart coming along the road, and heard someone say, 'It Mr Solomon. Good day, Mr Solomon.'

'Good afternoon, boys,' came the precise, familiar tones which Jason had never expected to welcome so warmly.

CHAPTER 15

A Case of Mistaken Identity

JASON was all ears, and heard one of the boys say:

'Mr Solomon, we done catch a spy!'

'Indeed?' said the old teacher.

'Yaas, Mr Solomon. He in de gatehouse. Dey done gone to telephone de police.'

'Please to stop to look at he, Mr. Solomon,' said Ramon.

'Thank you, I will.' The next moment Mr Solomon appeared on the threshold, dressed in his customary grey alpaca frock coat, white panama hat, white waistcoat and trousers. He stared in surprise at Jason sitting inside alone; and then, taking off his white-rimmed sun-glasses, he looked at him again.

'Good afternoon, my young friend,' he said. 'What are you doing here?'

Jason got up, and tried to speak, but his voice would not come. The crowd, however, eagerly answered for him.

'It de man Sambo see on de beach, Mr Solomon,' piped Goliah, the little boy whom Jason had first noticed. 'I done see him again dis afternoon comin' up from de beach.'

'Is Sambo here?' Mr Solomon asked, turning around and motioning the crowd to stand back.

'Sambo!' everyone shouted. 'Sambo! Come, man!' Sambo's foolish, frightened face peered round the door. Mr Solomon took him by the arm and pulled him forward.

'Now, Sambo,' he said, 'do you know who I am?'

'Yaas, Mr Solomon. Yo is de teacher, sah.'

'And do you think I tell lies?'

'No, Mr Solomon, you does speak de truth.'

'Very well. Now this man here,' he turned his white-rimmed spectacles towards Jason. 'Have you see him before?'

'Yaas, sah. On de beach.'

'When?'

'De day after Christmas, Mr Solomon, sah. He fire a gun. Bang! bang!'

'But . . .' Jason burst out, 'I wasn't . . . I . . .'

Mr Solomon held up a hand, and shook his head at him. 'You are quite sure, Sambo?' he asked.

'Yaas, de same man, Mr Solomon.'

'Now, Sambo,' he went on gravely. 'You know that this is a very serious charge to make. If a man is caught and proved to be a spy in war time, he may be shot. Do you still think he is the man who fired at you?'

Sambo rolled his eyes. 'I . . . I think so, sah. I dunno.'

'Come here, and pay attention, boys,' said Mr Solomon, gathering the ragged group about him. 'I want you all to hear this. Sambo, are you sure that this is the man you saw on the beach at Christmas time?'

'Yaas, sir,' the little boy Goliah screamed out. 'It de same man, sah.'

'Why, did *you* see him that day, as well as Sambo?' the old teacher asked.

Goliah shook his head, 'No, sah.'

The crowd was silent, looking uneasily at Jason.

'Now, see how easy it is to be mistaken,' said Mr Solomon. 'This is only a boy. He is an English boy. His name is Jason Foster. He is one of the pupils at Badanda College. He came here on the ship which was torpedoed in the harbour, and he was badly hurt, and has been ill in the College. He was nowhere near this island at Christmas time.'

'A mistake,' Ramon said. 'You's fault, Goliah.'

'Goliah done say it,' several voices said.

'Well, why he has a map?' Goliah wanted to know, with some defiance.

'Because I didn't know the island, and I wanted to find my way,' Jason said, finding his voice at last. 'I told them that I was from the College, but they wouldn't believe me.'

'They would far rather believe something exciting than the truth,' said Mr Solomon. 'Most unfortunate and unpleasant for you, but human nature. Now, Sambo, what have you to say? Is this the man you saw on the beach, and who fired at you?'

'No, Mr Solomon.'

'Then why did you say it was?'

'Goliah done say it, Mr Solomon.'

'But you said so too, yourself.'

'Goliah done say it, sah.'

'Now I've told you who this is, and you know that it is not the man you saw before.'

'Yes, Mr Solomon.'

'Goliah!'

'Yes, Mr. Solomon.'

'Who is this friend of mine?'

'He a College boy, Mr Solomon.'

'Are you sorry that you made this foolish mistake?'

'Yaas, sah,' said Goliah looking sulky, but added, 'Why he ran, den?' And the crowd echoed the question.

'He run away,' Ramon said. 'They was pitchin' stones, and I brought he here.'

'You did quite right, Ramon,' Mr Solomon shook his head reprovingly at the others. 'Stones! You might have hurt him.'

'Why he ran?' Goliah asked again, defiantly. 'If he ain't a spy, why he ran?'

'Wouldn't you run?' Mr Solomon asked, 'if you were chased by a crowd of people you didn't know?'

'But I see he comin' out of de cave on de beach, Mr. Solomon.'

'I had been resting there,' Jason explained. 'I had walked along the coast from the College, and was tired.'

'And Sambo, he seein' de man in de cave,' continued the boy Goliah.

'Yaas, sah!' Sambo interrupted with a wag of his foolish head. 'He done fire a gun, bang-bang!'

'Well, that wasn't me!' burst out Jason. 'Why do they go on saying this? I tell you, I've never been along this way before.'

'Let me deal with them, Foster,' the old teacher said. 'Now,' he continued, turning his back on Jason and wagging his finger at the two accusers while the crowd listened,

'The police will be here very soon, and will ask you what you have done to this young man. You boys are quite right to keep your eyes open. You are good boys, and you are loyal citizens. But if you find you have made a mistake you must apologize. This friend of mine was taking a walk by himself on the beach. He did not know the way, so he took a map, not thinking that it would make people suspicious. When you asked him who he was, he told you that he was from Badanda College. If you had not believed him you might have taken him across to Coconut Reach where the other schoolboys are. Instead, you chased him and threw stones at him. Luckily you did not hurt him, or the police might have taken you up, instead.'

'I . . . ain't done nuttin, Mr Solomon!' Sambo spluttered. 'I . . . I . . . I ain't even see he! Goliah say it.'

'Well, here are the police now,' Mr Solomon said. 'You must tell them that it is all a mistake, and that this is not the man you saw on the beach before, and that you are sorry for what you did. Do you understand?'

'Yaas, Mr Solomon,' Goliah said dolefully, as if he were sorry that the whole affair had turned out to be a mistake.

A car had stopped and the crowd, looking crestfallen and very disappointed, parted to allow two police officers to enter the lodge. One of them was Allen.

'Good afternoon, Mr Solomon,' he said. 'What's all this? Hello, Foster, what are you doing here?'

'It is a case of mistaken identity, sir,' Mr Solomon said in his careful voice. 'Our young friend was taking a walk by himself on the beach, and was mistaken for an alien.'

Allen burst out laughing, and after a moment of uncertainty the crowd began to laugh too. Only Sambo and Goliah looked abashed.

'Well,' Mr Solomon said, 'I am sure that Mr Foster will forgive you, but you must just say that you are sorry.'

'Sorry!' Sambo said, looking around for a chance to escape.

'Well, boys, it was a mistake,' said Allen, 'but one that can be understood.'

'I never thought I could run into trouble like this,' Jason cried.

'It was the map,' said Mr Solomon.

Allen nodded. 'Coming up from the beach with a map would make them suspicious ... I wonder ... Are you sure that the man you saw was anything like this boy?' he asked Sambo.

'I dunno, sah. Yaas, sah.'

'Did he have fair hair.'

'Yaas, sah.'

'But he was much older, wasn't he?'

'I dunno, sah.'

'How old are you?' Allen asked Jason.

'Fourteen,' Jason replied.

'Huh?' Goliah grunted. 'Fourteen? You tall, man!'

'He tall, eh?' the crowd said admiringly, taking Jason's side as quickly as they had leagued against him.

'And brave, too,' said Mr Solomon. 'Let me tell you what he did. He was on the ship when it was torpedoed, and he was badly hurt, but he took a smaller boy on his back and carried him all the way from the port to my house. For weeks afterwards he was ill. So really he carried the little boy to safety at the risk of his own life.'

Jason blushed brick red.

'What rot!' he muttered.

'Just let him speak,' Allen said to him in a low tone.

'So you see,' Mr Solomon went on, 'this brave English boy deserves praise instead of blame. Now we will show him how sorry we are for misjudging him by giving him three cheers.' He held up his hand. 'Hip, hip ...'

The negro crowd cheered with enthusiasm.

'I'll take you back to the College in my car,' Allen suggested.

'And I will go on my way,' Mr Solomon said. 'I have a visit to pay at the hospital. Good-bye, Mr Jason Foster. I will see you again.'

'Thank you, Mr Solomon,' said Jason. 'I owe you a lot.'

'I am pleased to have been of service, my young friend.

Now boys, you all have work to do. Go and do it. Good-bye.'
He waved them away, but it was not until the car had
driven off that they began to disperse.

'Well,' said Allen. 'That was an unfortunate adventure.
Were you hurt at all?'

'Oh no,' Jason replied quickly. 'They threw stones, and
I got one on the shoulder, and got the wind up. It was
stupid to try to bolt for it.'

'It was a good thing Old Solomon arrived when he did,'
Allen said. 'Besides, those people have long memories, and
are very hard to shake in their opinions. They would have
thought you a spy to the end of time if he had not proved
to them, there and then, how wrong they were.'

'I'd better come along with you to explain to Mr Boomhill,' he went on, 'It's really rotten luck and may rather
spoil your stay here. Don't be surprised if you are stared
at and whispered about.'

'I never wanted to come out here in the first place,' Jason
said wearily. 'And now, just as I was beginning to get used
to it, this happens.'

'Cheer up. There are worse places in the world to-day.
Oh – and a word of advice: go around with your friends,
and not alone. If you're in a crowd no one will pick you out.
Here we are ... And there's old Boomhill's car turning in
ahead.'

CHAPTER 16

The Special Messenger Seeks Advice

To Andrew nothing in the world was more enjoyable than a picnic, and this all-day outing at Coconut Reach should have made him the happiest boy alive. But strange to say he was uneasy in his mind. He wandered away from his three best friends (though they were no longer the Secret Four) and found himself staring out to sea. John was swimming, and in any case might not have been in the mood to hear confidences. The currents on this side of the island were too strong for any but the best swimmers, but there was an old lighthouse tower to climb, fish to be angled for from the rocks, and donkeys to be raced down the immense length of white sands. There were other diversions, too. Mr Jones was superintending a fish grill under the coconuts, and the boys were toasting yams for lunch. Immense quantities of ice-cream had been carefully stowed under straw to keep it from melting.

Lunch was marvellous, eaten in the shade of the coconuts with the trade wind stirring the great fronds above. Even with the great weight of worry on his mind Andrew found his appetite equal to the feast. Afterwards everyone lay about on the warm sand in nests which they scooped out for themselves. Mrs Grant had been bathing, and was preparing to rest with Jean, Guy and Pat; but Pat had made a conch horn out of shell, and was making loud booming noises on it, so she asked them to go a little farther off if they felt compelled to be noisy. So they went down the beach to practise. Guy made up his mind to walk along the trunk of a fallen coconut, balancing with outstretched arms like an acrobat. Andrew took the opportunity to go and sit beside Mrs Grant.

'I'd like to ask you something,' he began.

'What is it,' she answered pleasantly; but she was only half listening, for her eyes were on Guy.

'Supposing,' he said, 'Supposing ... that you thought there was some sort of danger, and you didn't know what to do about it ...'

'There's no danger here,' Mrs Grant said. 'You mustn't go around worrying about things, Andrew.'

On the beach at Coconut Reach

'But there might be,' Andrew faltered. 'If you thought that someone might be in danger ...'

'Never cross bridges until you come to them,' she replied lazily. 'Surely you are not going to turn into a worrier, are you? Especially not at a picnic ... Wait, Guy, Mummie will help you down!' She sprang up, and left Andrew disconsolate.

'Yoho, Andrew! We've found some sea grapes! Ripe ones!' Robin shouted, beckoning from the top of the lighthouse rock. So Andrew rejoined his friends who started to climb down a crack in the cliff after the greeny-yellow fruit. The sweet-salt mildness of the sea-grapes was pleasant even after a large lunch, and for a time he forgot his troubles, and climbed and picked as eagerly as anyone.

Then, suddenly, he thought of Lady May, and wondered why he had not remembered her before. She had said he was to be her Special Messenger, and had told him to keep his eyes open. That had been about migratory birds, to be sure ... But she might have been thinking of other things as well. It might only be a grown-up idea of a joke, but he made up his mind to try her. While the other boys were still climbing about, he went the other way, and soon a mass of rock separated him from them. If he cut through the coconut grove he thought he would reach the road along which the buses went to town. He began to run and was soon out of sight of the picnic party.

It was easy, in such a grove, to lose all sense of direction, for all the coconut palms seemed alike, though they drooped at different angles. Their fronds against the blue sky were never still: like the great green vanes of crazy windmills they wheeled about. No matter where he looked, he saw long, pale aisles, all alike, between the trunks, with occasional brown, rotting fronds that had fallen off, and over which he had to step. It was a little frightening; but as Andrew had once boasted to Goldbeard, he was good at finding his way. He could still make out a faint shimmer, which meant the sea, behind him; and by noticing carefully the way the sunbeams slanted whenever he reached a clearing, he made sure that he was at least not going in circles.

After a long time he saw a darker line amongst the palms, and found that he was coming to an embankment which marked the edge of the grove. He was so pleased, and relieved, that he sat down and rested for a while before climbing the bank and looking about for the road. Then he became aware of voices quite near by. At first he sat still, then started to crawl cautiously up the bank. There was a prickly hedge at the top, an effective barrier of thorny bougainvillea, which had been pruned until it was thick and strong, with great wicked-looking thorns as large as a boy's thumb. Looking through this thicket Andrew saw a car drawn up by the side of the road directly below him; and Goldbeard was changing a rear tyre. He was being helped by a bald-headed, sunburnt man whom Andrew had not seen before. Standing on a small hillock on the far side of the road was a young, fair-haired man a little taller than Jason. He seemed to be looking out over the countryside, and from time to time he called down a remark to the others.

Andrew looked and listened for a time, and then began softly to crawl along the bank, searching for a gap in the thorny hedge. About fifty yards to the right he came upon a ditch which made a sort of tunnel under it, and through this he crawled. A slight bend in the road hid him from the car and the watcher up on the hillock. Not one of them heard him coming up in his rubber shoes till he called out:

'Hello, Mr Dix, had an accident?'

Goldbeard's head came up quickly.

'Hello! What the ... Well, it would be you, wouldn't it?' He did not sound particularly pleased. The other two men were silent and stared at him. Andrew grinned in his most friendly manner. He looked more monkeyish than ever. In his khaki shorts and shirt and bare brown legs. His glasses were dusty, and he took out his handkerchief to polish them.

'How in the world did you manage to get out into this part of the island?' Dix went on, never stopping his work. He was now tightening the nuts all round the hub.

'We're having an all-day picnic at Coconut Reach,' Andrew said.

'Are you indeed?'

'Yes, but I just thought of something I wanted to do in town, so I thought I'd come on to the road and wait for a bus,' Andrew said, glancing at the car which could easily carry another passenger.

'I strongly advise you to go back to your picnic,' Dix said.

'If you are missed they might think you'd been drowned, and be put to a lot of trouble. Good-bye.' He finished tightening his nuts, threw the jack into the back of the car, said something to the other two who got in, and without an invitation to his small friend, drove off.

Andrew stared after them. It was quite possible that he might be missed, though not yet. In any case, he had made up his mind to see Lady May, and nothing else mattered for the moment. He decided to follow the car and watch for a lift. After about half an hour he came to a crossroad, and was lucky enough to see a bus coming. It was a small, rattle-trap affair with wooden seats which looked as though they had been made from orange crates, but Andrew got in, and bounced merrily along. He found that the money in his pocket was only just enough to take him into town. He would have none to bring him back again. This did not worry him very much.

He had not been through the port since the day of the fire. Now it seemed all different somehow. The streets which had been crammed then with frightened people were sleepy and deserted at this, the hottest part of the day. The wooden shops were largely repaired or rebuilt. The bus rattled through the business section and stopped at a place called Monument Square. Here a tiny river flowed into the sea, and the mouth of it was lined with stone quays at which the sailing sloops which plied between the Islands tied up. Beyond were the wharves for steamships. Andrew felt sorry that he had not time to see if they had hauled the torpedoed ship out of the harbour entrance.

This was the terminus, and Andrew looked about for someone to tell him the best way to Government House. Facing the square were large Government buildings made of stone, the Post Office and Customs House and other offices, but he did not think that Lady May would live in any of them. Spanning the little river, and leading into a beautiful road over which flowering trees arched, was a bridge. A large black policeman was directing traffic over it, and towards him Andrew went.

'Good afternoon,' he said politely, 'can you direct me to Government House, please?'

'Straight over de bridge,' the policeman answered, 'and foller de road. Goin' to walk dere?'

'Yes,' Andrew answered brightly.

'A long walk,' the man said, shaking his head. 'Better to take a bus.'

'I'm a good walker,' Andrew said, 'thank you,' and started briskly off.

All the same, when he was well on his way under the flowering trees which were like bright red parasols opened over him, he was glad of their shade. It might be miles and miles, and supposing Lady May were out? But here Andrew's incredible luck held, for at that very moment he got a lift, and from Lady May herself. She came driving along in her cream-coloured car, and Andrew waved frantically. Lady May recognized him in spite of the dust, and pulled up at the side of the road. As Andrew caught up, Lady May leaned out and beamed at him.

'Well,' she exclaimed, 'I do believe it's my special messenger! Have you been watching out for the migratory birds? Are you alone? And where are you going?'

'I was going to see you,' Andrew replied.

'Oh, were you?' Lady May replied, as if rather surprised. 'How delightful! But ... actually I was going out for the afternoon. If it's important, of course ... I mean, what you were coming to see me about?'

'Yes, it is, rather,' Andrew said. He longed to shout that it was frightfully important, but the eyes of the chauffeur were regarding him as if he were rather a problem, and for about the first time in his life he felt uncomfortable.

'Look here,' Lady May said suddenly to the man, 'Take the car along to the other entrance of the Botanic Park, and drive around twice, slowly, while Andrew and I have a little talk here on the bench inside the gates. Will that do, Andrew?'

'Yes, thank you,' Andrew answered. He was rather disappointed, because he had had dreams of going into a

'Is it important?' asked Lady May

private sitting-room at Government House, and even, perhaps, being invited to tea. But at least he was with her. She led him to a pretty sheltered hollow surrounded by a ring of nutmeg trees, where there were benches in the shade. It was too early for many visitors to be in the park. Only a few children were playing on the grass by the bandstand, and there was a gardener cutting hibiscus hedges with a cutlass, slashing strongly and yet lazily with sweeping movements of his whole arm.

'Now,' she said as she sat down, bending her head close to him, 'What is it? And why are you out all by yourself?'

'The other boys are at Coconut Reach,' Andrew said.

'Of course, for the all-day picnic. But that's a long way away! Didn't you go with them?'

'I did,' he answered. 'But then I took a bus up to the Port.'

'You asked permission first, of course?'

'No, I just came.'

'Dear me! Then it must have been important!'

'It is,' Andrew said solemnly, and found he could not go on. He blinked through his spectacles, rubbed his ears, swallowed, and finally stared helplessly at the sandy path.

'Have you got into some sort of trouble?' Lady May inquired. It occurred to her that the funny little fellow might be homesick, and had run away from school.

'It's not me that's in trouble,' he began. 'It's ... That's what I wanted to ask you. Supposing someone ... someone we like, was in trouble, or danger, or ... or ... perhaps worse, what should I do?'

To his great relief Lady May did not laugh or tell him not to be silly. An odd gleam came into her eyes for a moment, almost as though she shared his secret. Then she said slowly, 'You mean ... someone that we all know ... not a hundred miles away from the school, let us say?'

'Yes,' said Andrew. He was sure now that she knew, and the relief was so great that tears came into his eyes.

'Well, if I were you,' Lady May said, as if she were

weighing every word carefully, 'I would keep my eyes open, but say nothing. There are people here, you know, to take care of ... let us say ... this person ...'

'But if he needed a warning at any time ...'

'Andrew, there are some things which can't be explained until a long time after we know them,' Lady May said. 'Especially in difficult times like this. But be sure that this ... this special danger is, or rather, may be, provided for. How you know about it I can't imagine. But ... promise me this ... Don't try to do anything by yourself. If you feel that there is any sort of danger when no one else is there, well ... just stick to him. If all of you who came out together, let us say, stick close, quite close to him, like a sort of body-guard ...'

'But would he let us?' Andrew asked, rather taken aback.

'But why not? He'd be delighted, I'm sure.'

'Are you?' said Andrew. He blinked. He was not at all sure. But Lady May should know.

'Quite, quite sure,' Lady May said emphatically. 'These rather shy people often need companionship badly.'

'I wouldn't call him exactly shy,' Andrew said.

'Ah, but people don't always show their real feelings. He may be longing for friendship.' She hesitated, and then said in a low, rapid tone, almost as if she should not say anything about it. 'And, Andrew, I'll tell you in confidence, that the time of this danger may be shorter than you think. You may not have to worry long.'

'That's a good thing,' Andrew said. He felt greatly relieved at having got his worry off his chest. Lady May evidently knew what he meant, and knowing that she knew made all the difference.

'And now you must get back to the picnic,' Lady May said, 'before you are missed. I tell you what – I'll send you back in my car. Come, let's walk to the gate. There's the car coming round again now.'

'Oh, thanks awfully,' Andrew said, thankful that he had not had to ask for his fare back.

'Here we are,' she said as the car drew up. 'Hop in,

Andrew. I'm going to ask you to take me to the club first,' she remarked with a smile, 'and then the car will take you on to Coconut Reach.'

They drove to the Yacht Club, and stopped under the portico.

'Good-bye, Andrew,' Lady May said as she got out. 'And remember what I said. Stick close. Good-bye.'

In a car like that one, he would usually have had plenty to say, but all the way to Coconut Reach, he was silent. He was puzzled. He had never thought of Goldbeard as *lonely*. Outside the entrance to the grove the car stopped, and the man asked if Andrew would mind walking the rest of the way, as the sand was bad for the tyres. Andrew thanked him for the ride, and found his way back to the beach quite easily. No one had missed him, and it was time for tea.

CHAPTER 17

Who is the Spy?

'REALLY,' Mr Boomhill said, 'it was one of the funniest things I ever heard. To think that one of my own boys should have been taken for a spy, and brought home by the police!'

He was in an unusually genial mood. His scalp and eyebrows kept their proper places, and he laughed loudly and really heartily. The masters and boys who had just got back from Coconut Reach laughed too. It really was a splendid joke at Jason's expense.

'Next time, my lad, you'll go with your schoolmates instead of taking a solitary walk,' Jason was informed with a heavy pat on the shoulder, and his scowl brought from the Head, in a loud aside to Mr Jones, 'The boy's got no sense of humour! His father was a different sort. Always ripe for fun. The times we used to have ...'

The boys crowded round Jason, asking questions, all but John and Andrew. John stood apart and looked over the heads of the smaller boys, and from his glance Jason knew that their quarrel was over.

'But what was it all about?' asked Mrs Grant. She was in a hurry to put Jean and Guy to bed, but she felt that she must find out what had happened to one of the boys who had been in her charge.

'Why, Allen, the police officer, brought Jason home just now in his car,' Mr Boomhill chuckled. 'Old Solomon had rescued him from a mob of negroes who thought he was a spy. They saw him coming up from the beach with a map, and threw stones at him.'

'Are you hurt, Jason?' Mrs Grant and Miss Hall asked anxiously.

'No,' he replied coldly.

'What a good thing Mr Solomon happened to be

there,' Mrs Grant exclaimed. 'It might have been very serious.'

'Well, I think we'd better all get our hands washed and ourselves ready for supper,' Miss Hall said. She could see that Jason was upset, and needed to be rescued from the small boys who were pestering him.

As they moved off, Jason caught John by the arm. 'Come out into the garden. I want to talk to you.' They crossed the lawn to the bench at the end and sat down. Neither noticed Andrew behind them in the bushes.

'What a rotten thing to happen, Jass old son!' John said in his old, friendly way.

'It was beastly! I didn't know what they meant, all crowding round me. One of them kept swearing he had seen me before on the beach. I can't think what he meant.'

'I can,' said a shrill voice behind them.

'What are you doing there?' Jason cried furiously.

'I wanted to talk to you,' said Andrew.

'Well, we don't want to talk to you. Get out!'

'Look, you two,' Andrew said, coming out of his hiding place and standing before them. 'This isn't fooling. It's serious. Because I know why they thought it was Jason.'

'Thought who?'

'The real spy. You don't know what I've done to-day.'

'Eating most of the time, from what I could see,' John suggested. But there was something about Andrew that made Jason want to see what he had to say.

'I went to see Lady May.'

'What a yarn!' exclaimed John.

'I did, I tell you,' Andrew insisted, and proceeded to tell how he had found his way through the coconut groves and had heard voices. 'It was Goldbeard,' he said, 'and two men. They were changing a tyre. And they were all talking German.'

There was a dramatic pause.

'How do you know? You can't speak German,' John said.

'That's all you know,' Andrew said unexpectedly.

'Well, can you?'

'Yes, I can.'

'Well, you've never told us so before.'

'I don't tell you everything I know,' Andrew said indignantly.

'Don't you?' Jason said with mild sarcasm: 'It only seems like it then, I suppose.'

'Well, if you want to know,' Andrew said, 'I had a German governess. And before the war I used to go to Germany for holidays because my father's ships used to go to Hamburg.'

'Well, what about these men?' John asked. 'Did you see them close to?'

'Yes,' Andrew went on eagerly. 'I took a good look at them before I went down to the road. One was a bald-headed old man, rather sunburnt. The other was a bit like Jason, only older and taller – I mean his hair was yellow like yours.' He waited for Jason to object, but as he did not, went on: 'Afterwards, I crawled through the drain into the road, and went up and spoke to Goldbeard. I hoped he'd give me a lift.'

'Did he?' asked John.

'No. Of course I didn't tell them that I had listened to them talking. I just told Goldbeard I was looking for a bus.'

'I don't believe you,' John said. 'You are making all this up.'

'No, it is true,' Jason said unexpectedly. 'I saw them, too.'

'You did?' John and Andrew exclaimed together.

'Yes. They came out of Goldbeard's grounds in the car, and drove past me while I was with the mob.' He told them how he had seen the men pushing the boat, and how later they had gone by in the car with Dix driving.

'Then why didn't your mob recognize this other man, the one who was something like you, in the car?'

'Well, I suppose as he was with Dix, and they all know Dix, they sort of took him for granted.'

'Perhaps, yes ... but why on earth should such a man as that have been with Goldbeard?'

'I don't know,' Jason said. 'I hate thinking about it. It's rotten being taken for a spy, and having people looking at you like that. It's worse than having things thrown at you ...'

'But I haven't finished,' Andrew interrupted him impatiently. 'After they had gone I took a bus along to town, and I asked a policeman the way to Government House, and as I was walking there I saw Lady May, in a car, and I waved to her as I was going to see her anyway ...'

'What cheek!' said John.

'I was going to tell her about Goldbeard.'

John raised a sceptical eyebrow.

'That wasn't the only thing I was going to tell her about,' Andrew went on, 'I was going to ask her advice. John and I both saw him with that transmitter ...'

'What do you mean?' Jason asked irritably.

'Didn't you tell him, John?' Andrew asked.

'No.'

'John and I saw him with that transmitter that was found in the treasure hunt,' Andrew explained. 'We saw him bury it among the leaves.'

'So that's why you wouldn't go sailing with him!' Jason cried.

'Yes,' said John. 'Well, get on,' he said to Andrew.

'Well, so I waved, and she stopped, and I said I wanted to speak to her about something private, and she sent the car on, and we went into the park and sat down and talked.'

'You have more cheek than anyone I know,' John said.

'Twice as much,' Jason agreed.

'So we talked,' Andrew said, elated to see the impression he was making. 'I didn't mention Goldbeard's name, of course. I just said that supposing someone we all liked was in danger, what should I do about it. And what do you think? I could tell at once that she knew about it.'

'How could you tell?'

'By the way she listened, and what she said. She said things often can't be explained until afterwards. And she said that the danger was likely to be shorter, and come to an end quicker than I might imagine.'

'What did she mean by that?'

'I don't know. Perhaps the police know about Goldbeard, and are going to arrest him.'

'I don't believe he is a spy,' Jason said emphatically. 'I just don't believe it.'

'I like him as much as you do,' said John, 'but we did see him with that transmitter?'

'Anyway,' Andrew continued, 'I asked her what we could do about it. She said that supposing it was someone not a hundred miles from the school ... That's what she said, "Supposing it concerns someone not a hundred miles from the school ..." And you know that Goldbeard's house is much closer than that. It's not more than a couple of miles.'

'Get on, you nitwit!' Jason said.

'Well, I asked what I should do if I thought the danger was very threatening, and she said that we should all stick together and stay with him as much as we could.'

'What the blazes! ...' John murmured.

'I said, "But would he like that?" And she said, "Of course he would," or something like that.'

'It sounds all wrong to me,' John said.

'Anyhow, she said we were to stick around,' Andrew announced, 'so I am going to. And you had better, you two.'

'If you hang around Goldbeard with that knowing look in your eyes,' Jason said, 'he'll sheer off when he sees you coming. Or knock your block off.'

'No he won't,' Andrew said. 'I'm going to be his friend again, like I used to be on board.'

'Heaven help him!' John murmured.

'Well, I don't know anything about it,' Jason said suddenly, as if he had made up his mind, 'but I'm not going to believe that Dix is a spy. I don't know why he is doing these things, and I felt awful when he went past me like that. But I know what I felt when Goliah and Sambo and the others thought I was a spy, and I don't believe that Goldbeard is. I don't know what he's up to, but I like him.'

'Then you'd better do what Lady May said, and stick to him,' Andrew said.

CHAPTER 18

A Strange Trip in a Speed-boat

As usual on Saturday afternoons, the lagoon was one seething mass of boys. They had hoped to go outside the reef in their yachts, but an order had been given against it, and there was some excitement when Dix came into the anchorage with his speed-boat.

'Give us a ride! Give us a ride!' they shouted, but he only waved his hand quite pleasantly and went straight over to the little pier where he tied up. He sprang out so nimbly that Andrew, who had been on the watch for him, did not have time to get to the steps before Dix caught him up.

'Where's John?' Goldbeard asked. 'I'd like to speak to him.'

'Up at the schoolhouse,' Andrew answered. 'He ... They haven't come down yet.'

With a brief nod, Dix went briskly towards the school, stopping for a moment at Mrs Grant's bungalow to call, 'Is Pat ready?'

'Yes,' she said. 'But he had to go up to the College to get his shoes.'

'I'll find him,' Dix answered, and continued on his way.

'Pat's not very keen on boating,' Andrew said, tagging along behind. 'Were you going to take him out in the speed-boat?'

'I thought I might.'

'He won't want to.'

'There's something wrong with the engine ... Nothing much, but it makes a little fuss. I thought he might like to watch it,' Dix replied.

Andrew thought over this. It seemed queer, but obeying Lady May's suggestion he followed close behind Goldbeard as he went across to the College verandah. Mr Boomhill was just going out, as he usually did on Saturday afternoons.

Andrew was amazed to see how his attitude to Goldbeard had changed. His eyebrows did not go up, and though there was still some perplexity in his glance, he seemed only too eager to be friendly.

'Anything you want?' he asked, pausing on the running-board of the car.

'No, thanks,' Dix answered. 'I just want to speak to John a moment.' Mr Boomhill waved his hand and drove off. John and Jason were coming down the stairs from the dormitory where they had been changing into their swimming things. Goldbeard greeted them in his friendly way. 'Hello, John,' he said. 'Like to go out with me in the boat?'

'And Jason too?' John asked, holding his friend's arm.

'Certainly,' Dix answered. 'Come on, then. Is Pat anywhere about?'

'I think he's with Miss Hall in his dormitory. I saw him as we passed.'

'I'll call him,' Andrew said with alacrity. He ran upstairs. His fingers and toes were tingling. He felt a little dizzy with expectation. Pat was standing by Miss Hall who seemed to be counting out clothes and looking to see if names were sewn on to Pat's things. 'Goldbeard ... Mr Dix ... wants to take Pat for a ride in his speed-boat,' Andrew gasped.

'Run along then, Pat,' Miss Hall said, as if it were the most ordinary thing in the world. Pat came obediently, going slowly and solemnly down the stairs while Andrew slid down down the banisters and waited impatiently at the bottom. Dix was laughing and talking with John and Jason, watching out of the tail of his eye for Pat, and when he saw him he went on talking, but held out his hand which Pat took without looking at him.

They all went down the hill together, Andrew following at Jason's heels. They went on to the pier. 'Will you steer, Jason?' Dix asked.

'If you think I can, well enough.'

'Sure you can! John, you sit in the stern ... That's right. Let Pat get in at the front ... Go carefully Pat, the boat's a bit damp, and those rubber shoes are apt to slip. Here, take them off and give them to me, I'll leave them here by the boathouse, and you can get them when we come back.'

'And I'll sit here,' Andrew said, stepping in uninvited.

'But I can't take you. You can't swim,' Goldbeard exclaimed.

'Yes I can. Anyhow, I can swim better than Pat. Oh, go on, let me! Please let me!' Andrew grinned disarmingly. He did not mean to desert his post. Goldbeard looked at his watch hastily.

'Oh, all right,' he said, as if he had no more time to lose. 'I'll take you if you'll do exactly as I say.'

'O.K.,' said Andrew.

Dix started the engine, and they went purring across the lagoon at a fine pace. A murmur of envy rose from the other boys. Andrew made rude, triumphant signs at them as they passed, but gave a regretful wave to Robin.

'Golly! Are we going outside the reef?' he cried. Dix did not answer, but as they approached the rocky entrance he slowed down; and when they were hidden by the great rocks from the view of those in the lagoon, he stopped for a moment, holding the boat still by catching hold of a projecting point of rock.

'Now listen,' he said in an almost harsh voice that they had never heard before. 'Each of you is to do exactly as I say. Andrew!'

'Yes,' said Andrew, astonished.

'Do you see that shutter on your side of the boat, near the floor?'

'Yes,' said Andrew, getting down and looking at it.

'Slide it along.'

'Golly!' said Andrew, 'there's a thick glass panel underneath. To see fish through, I suppose.'

'Yes, that's the observation panel. Now, if you'll promise to lie down on the floor and keep your eyes glued to it, I'll let you go with us. If not, I'll lift you out here on to the reef, and pick you up when we come back.'

Andrew did not much like the way he said it, but he promised, and lay down flat on the bottom of the boat.

'Don't get up once, or even lift up your head,' Dix said sternly.

'No, sir.'

'John!'

'Yes.'

'I want you to get over into the water. I'm going to tow you along to a certain point. We are going straight out to the end of the Five Fishers. When we come up to the last one I will give you a signal. Then let go of the boat and swim, under water, until you are close to shore. Make for the landward side of the last of the Five Fishers. In a small cove you will find a boat tied. Loose it, and see that it floats free of the shingle. There's a strong current running. Once it is in the fairway it should drift away quite fast. Then get back to shore. You can swim, or you can make your way along the islands. The tide's high still, though it is going out. Now and then you may have to swim. Keep down, so that you are not seen. Do you understand?'

'Yes, I think so, sir,' said John.

'Don't wait for us, you understand. Simply untie the boat, and then get back unobserved.'

'Yes, sir,' said John.

'Jason, steer as I tell you. We are going to run straight out beyond the end of the Fifth Fisher. Pat is going to sit up here in front with me where he can watch the engine.'

Of all of them Pat was the only one who did not seem aware that something strange was happening. He was in his turtle-like state of quietness. But when Dix took the cover off the engine, Pat's eyes at once sought the working pistons, and his face woke up. They went through long valleys of waves, bouncing occasionally; and Andrew squeaked as the spray came in.

'Oooh! there's a whole lot of little fish, swimming away as fast as they can go!' he exclaimed. 'There's a rock pretty close . . . Would it smash the glass panel if it touched?'

'It won't. The tide's too high,' Dix answered.

'Oh, there's a larger fish: a mackerel, or a king-fish. Oh, look at these ...'

'Keep your eye glued,' Dix said. He turned to Jason. 'We keep straight on our course until we reach the end of the last Fisher,' he said. 'Then we go beyond it for about fifty yards, north past the tip, and then turn back again. I will tell you exactly when to turn.'

The First Fisher was almost joined to the beach; the Second was larger, separated from the First by a channel about twenty yards wide. The Third was a little group of rocks and reefs, the Fourth, a long island overgrown with scrub, with a few spindly trees bent sideways by the wind. The Fifth Fisher was round, with a small hill on the shoreward side, and it was separated from the Fourth by a shallow channel. It was only when you were nearly at the end that a little hut became visible in a small grove of trees which, being sheltered from the wind by the hillock, grew straight and bushy.

When they reached the end of the Fourth Fisher Dix gave a low whistle, and John's hand disappeared from the side of the boat. Jason watched him swimming steadily under water in the direction of the shore.

'Look out for a couple of rocks to starboard,' Dix warned Jason. 'When we get out beyond the Fifth Fisher watch until you see them in a line with the island, and then pull your tiller, and we go north until I say the word. Then put her round, and run past the island again.'

They were now close to the island which, on the seaward side, seemed to be on a sort of ledge, with deep water beyond. The reefs which edged all the Five Fishers stopped at the last, and the water was blue instead of green. Jason was so busy looking out for the two rocks that he had no time for anything else until after he had changed the direction of the boat, and they were heading north.

Dix had slowed down, but the tide was running strongly, and the boat was carried past the furthest point of the island. Jason turned his eyes towards the shore. There were three people standing there among the trees. Though they

were within hailing distance neither they nor Mr Dix gave
any sign. One man was standing apart, with his arms so
wound about a tree that it looked almost as if he were tied
to it. Several paces behind him were the two others, and
Jason knew instantly that they were the ones he had seen
putting the smashed boat into Dix's boathouse, the same
he had afterwards seen with Dix in the car. He was so much
disturbed by this that for an instant he took his hand off
the tiller. The boat lurched, and Andrew's head came up
like a weighted toy for a brief, surprised look over the side
to see what it was all about.

'Steady, Jason,' Dix said sharply. He put out his foot and
pushed Andrew's head down again without ceremony.
Andrew lay looking up sideways through his glasses trying
to read Goldbeard's expression. His heart beat fast. He
tried not to be frightened, and was comforted to see Jason
staring straight ahead. He could not really be afraid in
Jason's company.

'You stand up here, Pat, where you can see better,' Dix
said. 'This is the throttle. You work it ... like this.' Pat
stood up, facing the shore, his eyes fixed on the engine. Jason
could see that the man by the tree was looking at the boat
through field-glasses which another man held before his
eyes. Then they were beyond the island, and Dix gave the
order to put about. Once more they passed the tip of land,
but not before Jason had seen, diminishing in the distance,
what might easily have been a small boat adrift. Now, as
they went south, the tide ran strongly against them. Dix
had lifted Pat to the other side of the boat, so that he faced
the island again as they passed. 'Now, straight for home,'
he said in a changed voice. 'Move over, Jason, and let me
steer. I know the entrance to the lagoon.' Pat still stood
watching the engine, and Dix's eyes rested on him with a
curious expression. Jason, looking from one to the other,
could not follow what was going on. As they passed them,
he also looked at each of the Fishers in turn, but he could
see nothing of John. He'll be all right, he told himself. He's
a good swimmer. But he was worried for all that.

They could see three people standing by the trees

'I'm beginning to feel sick seeing things go by so quick,' Andrew complained.

'Get up if you like, now,' Dix said casually. Andrew immediately sprang up.

'You might let me steer a little, I think,' he said. 'I've not seen anything except fishes since we started.'

'There's a bag of lollipops in the locker,' Dix said unexpectedly with his boisterous laugh. 'You might take charge of them, for your Secret Stores, you know.' He laughed again, and Andrew laughed, too. He felt that a cloud had lifted. Jason's face relaxed, and he graciously accepted a lollipop. Even Pat looked up and smiled.

They went back to the lagoon, and Dix made fast to the pier, gaily shaking his head at the other boys who surrounded them, begging to be taken out.

'Tea-time,' he said, and chased them off.

John came strolling down the sand in his wet bathing suit. Dix looked at him inquiringly.

'O.K.,' John said.

Goldbeard nodded. He laid an arm on John's shoulders, drew Jason towards him, and even included Andrew with a smile.

'This is secret,' he told them. 'Nothing to be said. Understand?' They nodded. 'Tea-time,' he said again. 'Let's see, Pat, we threw your shoes by the boathouse. Here they are. Shove your feet in. There! Take Pat's other hand, Jason, and we'll give him a giant's stride up the steps together. One, two, three! ... and we're off!' He took one of Pat's hands, and Jason took the other, and the little boy took flying leaps up the hill between them. Andrew followed breathlessly behind, and John came slowly, last.

'Bravo!' a cheerful voice greeted them, and there was Lady May clapping her hands, with Mrs Grant and Miss Hall standing with her. 'That was a fine spurt up,' she continued. 'It did me good to look at you.'

'Yes, Dix, old man,' said Mr Boomhill in his most genial voice, 'I doubt whether even twenty years ago I could have taken those steps at a better pace myself! We'll have to time ourselves one day.'

'What's the matter, Pat?' Mrs Grant asked, for he was limping a little.

'A bit of gravel in my shoe,' Pat said in his even voice. He bent over and took it off, shook it – and a large scorpion fell out.

There was a horrified silence on the verandah. Then old Millie, who had come down the stairs, said, in an awed voice:

'That a child of God, sure. He a child of God. He go far! He go very far!'

Pat pulled his shoe on again. Mr Boomhill put his heel on the scorpion, crushed it, and kicked it off the verandah.

'Better to burn he,' Old Millie said, and went to the kitchen for some tongs.

'Let me look at your foot, dear,' Miss Hall said in a trembling voice, taking Pat on her lap. 'It didn't bite you, did it?'

'No,' said Pat.

'I suppose it would have been fatal to a child of that age?' Mr Jones said in a scared tone.

'Absolutely,' Dix said. He had sat down suddenly. His face had gone so white that his beard and hair looked positively fiery. 'What might have happened!' he gasped, 'and at this juncture!'

'At the very last moment!' added Mr Boomhill solemnly.

'But it didn't happen,' said Lady May, her voice cheerful as usual.

'What's it all about?' asked Andrew on the outskirts.

'A scorpion in Pat's shoe,' Jason replied.

'Yes, a black scorpion,' Old Millie said. 'Look out, chile, I gettin' he to burn.'

'What are you going to do with it? Oh, I say, it's the biggest one I've ever seen!'

'It goin' to burn,' said Old Millie, stalking away with it.

'Oh, Millie, give it to me to put into my museum. I'll pickle it in a bottle. Oh, come on, Millie!'

'I goin' to burn he!' Millie repeated obstinately, and disappeared into the kitchen quarters, with Andrew following her.

CHAPTER 19

The Mystery Solved

As Old Millie took the skillet off the firepot and cast the scorpion into it Andrew remembered Lady May's injunction that he was to stick to the others. He scurried back to the verandah, but the two older boys were nowhere to be seen. Lady May's car was still parked in the drive, but she was not on the verandah. Andrew ran softly upstairs, but the only person he saw was Miss Hall who was busily packing a small trunk.

'Hello, Miss Hall,' Andrew said. 'Have you seen John and Jason?'

'Not in the last five minutes,' Miss Hall answered. She picked up a label and tied it on to the trunk. Under Pat's name was written, 'Ottawa, Canada.'

'Why are you packing Pat's things? Is he going away?' he asked.

'Oh, Andrew,' Miss Hall said,' go down and tell Dinah to bake some jam tarts for supper to-night, will you? I forgot.'

Andrew stared at her, and departed. He looked suspiciously about him as he went, but could see nothing of his friends. However he saw Dix's car moving away from the porch, and wondering if John and Jason were inside he ran after it. It was getting dusk now, and he ducked below the level of the verandah hoping that no one would see him. At the end of the drive the car stopped, and Andrew, peeping through a vine, saw that Dix was alone in it. Two other cars were out there on the main road. One, a Government lorry, was full of men in uniform; and the other was Allen's car.

'O.K.?' Allen called.

'Right!' Dix answered.

Allen got back in his car and it moved slowly along, with the lorry following. Dix's car disappeared in the opposite direction, which led to town. Andrew, keeping in the shadow of the bushes, tiptoed after the two cars which were going without headlights slowly towards the church. At the gap in the hedge where the path marked the end of the College property they stopped. The uniformed men got out and, with Allen, disappeared down the hill. Andrew watched them creeping down the steep cliff between the rocks and bushes. At the base of the hill, opposite the First Fisher, a line of scrub grew like a hedge along the beach. Behind it, the soldiers sat down as if waiting for someone. Allen was with them.

Without a sound Andrew crawled along the path leading back to the College grounds. He must find John and Jason, whatever happened. It was now so late that the other boys must have come up from the lagoon and were probably in the playroom, but John and Jason were not there. Andrew rushed back to the beach. The pavilion was empty, so were the bathing huts. Then he heard a door slam in the boathouse, and saw them coming slowly along.

'Hurry, you two,' he said in a breathless whisper. 'Where have you been?'

'What's that to you?' John asked.

'Come on, you muts! You must come!'

'Come where?'

'You don't know what I've seen!' Andrew panted. 'Soldiers! They're waiting over there at the foot of the cliff path. Allen is with them.'

'Soldiers?' Jason echoed.

'Just opposite the First Fisher . . . Hiding behind the bushes.'

'Of course!' John gave a sort of whistle. 'Now I see. The men you saw on the island would have to walk to the shore, because that was their boat I pushed off.'

'It will be low tide soon,' Andrew said.

'If the soldiers are waiting for them,' Jason said, 'it must be a trap. But why did Dix want to take Pat in the boat?'

'Didn't you see who was on the island with those two men?'

'Yes. I saw the two men who were with Dix in the car that day.'

'But the other one!' whispered Andrew in tremendous excitement. 'I think I'm beginning to see . . . I think I do.'

'The other man I didn't know,' Jason said slowly, 'though it does seem to me I've seen his face before.'

'You have, and you haven't,' muttered Andrew, mysteriously. 'But don't stay here wondering. We've just got time to get up there before they come across. Hurry!'

Without another word the two older boys followed Andrew up the steps past Mrs Grant's bungalow. They could hear her inside reading a bedtime story to Jean. It was almost time for the first bell.

'Keep down,' whispered Andrew, 'Don't let them see us from the school, or they'll fetch us in. Get behind these bushes, and we'll get past the kitchen without being seen.' They could hear Dinah and the other servants talking as they passed. Old Millie was relating the story of the scorpion in Pat's shoe for the hundredth time.

'I say, he a child of God!' she repeated, and the others marvelled with her.

Andrew crawled rapidly between the bushes into the old hiding-place of the Secret Four. By lifting a branch of gorse he made a sort of window through which they could look down on the soldiers so still and silent below. They were not smoking. No one could possibly have guessed they were there.

'Look! Look!' Andrew breathed. 'They're coming across.'

The tide was out, and the wet sand was still red from the sunset though the sun had disappeared into the sea. Across the narrow channel from the First Fisher three men came wading. The one in the middle was secured by a rope which was held by the others. Jason put his hand over Andrew's mouth, but he was clenching his teeth, and shook his head to show that he had no intention of making a sound. Still the watchful men behind the bushes remained motionless. The three men reached the firm sand. The first, a shorter man, pointed northwards along the beach. The third nodded. The one between, who walked along like a bear between keepers, said nothing.

Then suddenly it happened. When they were level with them, on the other side of the bushes, the armed men

Three men came wading across the channel

sprang on them. The first and last were seized. There was no firing. The man in the middle did not attempt to run. They could see Allen cutting the rope that bound his arms. Then the soldiers were coming up the hill with their two prisoners. Jason gently let the furze branch go back into place, and the three boys held their breath as the men went by. There was a subdued tread of feet on the paved road above, and then the sound of the lorry being started up. It drove away.

Allen and the other man came slowly up the hill.

'Well, how you managed it I cannot think,' the stranger was saying.

'It was Dix who planned everything,' Allen replied.

'When I saw Pat in the boat this afternoon, it was a nasty shock,' the stranger said. 'I didn't know what they meant when they said that they would persuade me to change my mind about working for them. When I saw Pat I understood. They thought that he was in their power. Of course they had no idea that I knew Dix. As soon as I saw him I knew everything would come out all right, though I did not know how.'

'It must have been a dangerous moment when they discovered that the boat was gone,' said Allen.

'Yes, that was a bad five minutes. I almost thought they were going to kill me when they found it had gone. But of course that would have put an end to their plans for making me work for them.'

'I don't know how it was managed,' Allen said. Andrew squeezed John's arm. 'Let's wait here for a moment,' he continued. 'Lady May is coming in her car, with Pat, to pick you up.'

'Is this the school grounds?' the man asked.

'Just in there. But we don't want to set the servants talking. You are both to spend the night at Government House, and a plane's calling for you to-morrow morning.'

'What about the submarine ...?'

'That's all right,' Allen said.

'But they used a transmitter to speak to it. Of course they could only send messages, not receive.'

'We've got that,' said Allen.

'They haven't captured the submarine already?'

'Yes. One of our seaplanes had been lurking on the other side of the peninsula where they put in. When you three had left and were well out of sight it flew over and dropped depth bombs all around it. The sub came up in a hurry, and the plane took it prisoner.'

'You're joking!'

'Fact! The first time in history that it's been done, I believe. Good fun! A couple of destroyers came and took it over. So that's all right. We had a particular interest in that submarine. Before they took you on board they sank a steamer in the entrance to the harbour here, the ship that Pat came out on, and Dix.'

'Good heaven!'

'At least, I shouldn't say that Dix was on board, for he wasn't. We took him off during the night when the steamer was standing off shore.'

'Did he know it was going to happen?'

'No. It was too good an opportunity for them to miss, I suppose – the chance of sealing up our harbour. The strange thing is that no one seems to have noticed that Dix wasn't on board. Might have been awkward if they had.'

Andrew was wriggling with excitement. The other two held him.

'But what about the transmitter?' the stranger asked. 'They sent a message to the submarine.'

'It would be received all right . . . by our men. That transmitter nearly spoiled Dix's show. He had to bring it up once to see to something that was wrong. He left it somewhere about here in a pile of leaves intending to pick it up later, and some of the schoolboys found it in a treasure hunt. It caused a sensation, I can tell you. Made old Boomhill, the Headmaster, frightfully suspicious of Dix.'

'But why of Dix?'

'It's a long story . . . One of the boys picked up a newspaper which Dix had dropped. He got it from the enemy agent, in the course of one of their meetings, and the

Headmaster naturally wondered where it had come from. As a matter of fact he worried over it so much that he finally went to the Governor. Without revealing any secrets he gave him a hint as to the true state of affairs. Didn't make it any easier for Dix.'

'The men in the submarine used to laugh at the defences of these islands,' the stranger said. 'They used to boast that they came and went as they wished.'

'We let them have plenty of rope,' Allen said with a laugh. 'But it didn't follow that they were never noticed. As a matter of fact one of the schoolboys here was followed and taken up as a spy. Might have been nasty if he hadn't kept his head.' Andrew nudged Jason who nobly restrained himself from returning the prod.

'And is Pat all right?' the stranger asked.

'Quite all right. He never suspected his danger.'

'Is that the car now?'

'Yes. Come on. It's so dark that you'll need this torch ...'

They resumed their climb. The watching boys saw the headlights of a car advancing through the bushes. A car door opened. The stranger's voice said, 'Hello, Pat, is that you?' And Pat's voice, raised above its usual flat tone, called, 'Daddy!' The car door slammed, the engine purred, and the car was gone.

'Well!' Andrew exclaimed. 'Did you hear ...'

'Of course we heard!' Jason said.

'But you don't know, you muts, because I didn't tell you, that I saw Miss Hall packing Pat's trunk just a few minutes ago, and I saw a label on his trunk, and it said Ottawa, Canada. And I asked if Pat was going away, and Miss Hall asked me to go down and tell Dinah to have tarts for supper ... and, oh gosh! I forgot all about it.'

'Then that strange man,' John said, 'must be Pat's father.'

'Of course he is, you idiots,' Andrew exclaimed. 'Didn't you recognize him from the picture that's standing on Pat's dresser?'

'Of course, that's why he seemed familiar,' Jason said.

'I knew when I saw him on the island that I had seen his face somewhere.'

'I just caught a look at him when you made the boat lurch,' Andrew said. 'But Old Goldbeard pushed my head down with his foot. I wonder why?'

'Because, you silly tripe-hound, you had gone and stared at them when Dix was changing the tyre. He didn't want them to think that you were a friend of his.'

'Of course, that's it,' Andrew murmured. 'And, oh gosh! when Lady May said that about a person not a hundred miles away, she meant Pat, not Goldbeard. She thought I meant that Pat was in danger. That's why she said to stick to him. What a mix-up! I thought she was wrong to think that Goldbeard was shy. Crumbs!'

'If that was Pat's father,' John said, 'he is perhaps the greatest of British scientists. I wonder how he got here if he was a prisoner in Germany.'

'They must have got him out by submarine,' Jason said slowly. 'I think I see. They wanted him to do some scientific work for them, and he refused, and they found out that Pat was being sent here, and they thought they'd make him by getting hold of Pat.'

'But Pat was with Dix,' Andrew said.

'Stupid! They thought Dix was on their side, and could get Pat.'

'Did they?'

'Of course. That's why he was so worried when Pat was missing in the beginning,' John murmured.

'When he said the devils had got him ... I remember,' Andrew said eagerly. 'Oh, I wish we knew all about it! I'm going to ask him ...'

'He wouldn't explain, you goop!' Jason said. 'If he went around explaining, what good would he be as a counter-spy? That's why he wouldn't pick me up that time. He had to get those two off. And look here, Andrew ... don't you try to get away ... John, take hold of his other arm ... Look here, Monkey, you are never going to say anything about what has happened to-night. They didn't know we were listening. No one must know. They didn't even let Pat's father go to the school to get him because they thought the servants might notice that he was a stranger. Promise you will hold your tongue!'

'What do you think I am?' Andrew asked indignantly.

'A prattler,' John said lazily.

'I'm not. I know when to keep quiet.'

'You won't even tell your three playmates?'

'No, I won't even hint about it . . . I . . . I won't even look as though I had a secret.'

'Let him go,' John said, 'We'll just have to hope for the best.'

'The first bell went some time ago,' Jason said. 'By gum, it's dark! I can't see.'

'Hold on to me,' Andrew said with importance. 'I know this path with my eyes shut . . . Come on . . . I say, when Allen was telling Pat's father that he was quite all right, he didn't know about the scorpion, did he?'

'No, he wasn't there,' Jason answered. 'That's why Goldbeard was so upset. If anything had happened to Pat just then, when his father was coming to get him!'

'Did you hear what Old Millie said, that Pat was going far? Well, so he is . . . All the way to Canada.'

'She didn't mean that sort of far, you stupe,' John murmured.

'What did she mean then?'

'She meant that he was going to be a famous man, like his father.'

The second bell rang.

'You go on,' Andrew said. 'I must just stop in the kitchen and ask Old Dinah not to tell that I forgot to give the order for the tarts.'

'Hurry up, then,' Jason urged. As Andrew vanished Jason sighed and said, 'It would be Pat's luck to go to Canada. Why couldn't it have been me?'

'I suppose his father's going to do research work there,' John said. 'Pat will probably be a scientist too, when he grows up. He's always fiddling with machines and things.'

'He's a queer bird,' Jason said.

'And, like a bird, he's going to fly,' Andrew said appearing again. 'A migratory bird, if you lads know what that means,' he added.

When they reached the verandah everyone was streaming across to the dining-room. Andrew looked eagerly to see if Goldbeard was standing in his usual place, but he was not. Mrs Grant and Miss Hall were there, and Andrew could see that they were both looking pleased. Mr Boomhill's expression was curious. He seemed full of importance, and yet just the least bit annoyed. Mr Jones, standing behind him as usual, looked pop-eyed as if he had met something which had frightened him.

'Pat asked me to say goodbye to you,' Mrs Grant said to the three as they approached. 'He has gone to stay with some relatives.'

'Isn't he coming here to school any more?' Andrew asked with such elaborate innocence that Jason longed to give him a clout on the side of the head.

'I don't think so,' Mrs Grant answered.

'Just a moment,' Mr Boomhill said. He had a parcel under his arm. 'This is for you, Andrew,' he said. 'It is a stamp album from a man who doesn't need it any more. He wants you to have it.'

'Oh, thanks a million times,' Andrew said, astonished. 'But who . . .'

'Put it into your locker until after supper,' Miss Hall said. 'And you'd better hurry and wash your hands.'

'Just a word with you two,' Mr Boomhill said to Jason and John. 'I have been asked if I will allow you to receive a present from a friend. It is the little yacht which you have helped to put into order. I see no reason why you should not have it, especially as one of you has a taste for the sea. Would you care for it?'

'Rather!' John said. 'It's awfully good of . . . Thanks frightfully.'

'It's marvellous!' Jason said, his voice slipping up to the childish register which he hated.

'Very well, you may take delivery of her to-morrow. And I will myself test out your capacity for handling her.'

The two boys went upstairs to wash, and Jason said, 'It sounds as though we were not going to see Dix again. Do you suppose he's going away, too?'

'I wonder,' John answered, 'I hope not ... There's one thing, Jass old son,' he said as they were going down again. 'You wouldn't want to go away now, when we've got our own boat and all, would you?'

'No,' Jason said. 'No, I don't think I would.'